Presented to M

Janet McC......

by

Leda Boal

Berth Day Kake
Story Two of the Melt

Harv Boal

COCHRANTON PUBLIC LIBRARY
PO BOX 296
107 WEST PINE STREET
COCHRANTON PA 16314
814-425-3996
www.ccfls.org/cochranton

Copyright © 2015 John Harvey Boal III

All rights reserved.

ISBN: 1515255611
ISBN-13:978-1515255611:

DEDICATION

For Cubs and Cricket, who know that, indeed,
"the child is father to the man."

ACKNOWLEDGMENTS

The events of this story take place in a parallel universe during an alternate timeline. Characters and places may have similar names to those in our world, but they should not be confused with those of the Earth we know and inhabit.

Chapter 1

Different people react differently to terminal diagnoses. Bishop Brewan had noticed this many times back when he was a parish pastor. Sometimes, people were frozen when they were told they had only a short time remaining to live. Others acted with frenzy, trying to cram years of living into a few weeks or months. It depended upon the person, the circumstances, their mindset, and how ill they felt at the time. That was the way it worked with individuals. How, Bish wondered, was a whole world supposed to act when it received a terminal diagnosis?

As a boy, Brewan had read many science fiction stories about world disasters where populations journeyed into space in order to save humanity when Earth was doomed. Even though many of these stories had contained catastrophic elements, they had all been optimistic overall. They never ended with the world giving up. Their final chapters never said "and no one lived happily ever after." Yet, that seemed to be the way this story, the true story of the true world, was likely to come to conclusion. It made Bishop wonder.

It made him wonder about a lot of things. As the ocean impeded more and more upon the land, as freshwater supplies measurably shrank all over the world, as crowded populations desperately sought new places to settle, would there come a time when people just gave up? Or would the time come first when governments or groups or individuals did something so incredibly stupid that they hastened the demise of the creatures God created on the sixth day of creation?

The Rev. Dr. Bishop Bishop Brewan, Bishop to Southeast Alaska for the EPIC church, believed the promise that God had made after the Great Flood, the rainbow promise. He did not expect water to destroy the world again. Still, water seemed to be working very hard to make the planet something different from what it had ever been before.

"Come quickly, Lord Jesus," he prayed. "Come quickly, Lord Jesus."

Six weeks had passed, six weeks and two days to be accurate, since the anti-alcohol drug in his bloodstream had sent him into a seizure that nearly killed him. He still wasn't sure if taking the Cantabuse had been one of the best ideas of his life or one of the worst. Diane definitely had her opinion and his daughters had theirs and, of course, Jacob Jaegar had an opinion too. The Elder Director was chiding him on the phone again now as he tried to eat his lunch.

"Sometimes your stupidity seems to pass even the greatest expectations of all your friends and foes who actually know how stupid you are," said Jaegar.

"I love you too, Jake," said Bishop.

"That's not the point, Bish," said Bishop's boss. "You know that's not the point."

"What I know, is that it worked," said Bishop. "That's all that I really know. It succeeded and how can you argue with that success?"

That was certainly not a fair question. Bish knew it was not a fair question because Diane had told him that at least four or five times a day over the last six weeks. Nearly killing himself may have saved himself, in his eyes, but in the eyes of his wife nearly killing himself had nearly killed himself. That was all she needed to know.

"Hey," said Bish, "I have to go. Diane just came in."

"Let me say hi," said Jaegar.

"Okay, we'll talk soon," said Bish, hanging up the phone, because Diane had not just walked into the room. He would have let Diane and the Elder Director converse if she had really entered the room, but Bish did not expect her for at least another hour. He was just too tired to talk to Jaegar anymore, and he was more than tired of listening. His Pennsylvania grandmother, Granma Kaye, used to say, "There's no use of beating a dead horse." Bishop wasn't exactly sure what she meant by that, but it seemed like a saying appropriate to the situation. He closed his eyes and tried to go to sleep.

The doctors told Bish that he had lost nearly twenty-five pounds during that first week of dehydration, convulsion, and near kidney shutdown following his mishap on the outskirts of Muir. He must never, ever, take that drug again they told him. It would be suicide. And if it wasn't, Diane had assured him, then there would be a homicide so that the end results would be the same.

Bish laughed now at the memory of her seriousness and was relieved and surprised that laughter did not hurt the way it had for the first month. Apparently, his three cracked ribs were healing too. He had never known that you could break your own ribs by vomiting. Yet, he had never guessed that it was possible to almost turn yourself inside out either, but it had certainly felt that way on that afternoon a month and a half ago.

It had been a long month and a half. When the Coast Guard life-flighted Bish from Muir to Juneau they had done so with the full expectation that he would soon be transferred to the Lower 48 or to the local cemetery. There did not seem to be too many other options. He was a mess.

The doctors in Juneau had briefly considered sending him to Anchorage, but it was quicker and more efficient to aim for Seattle. Bish had overestimated Diane's arrival time in Southeast Alaska and she had, in fact, still been at SeaTac Airport when the news of his injuries reached her. She found him at Seattle Presbyterian Hospital within an hour of his arrival there.

Bishop Brewan's memories of the next few days were as cloudy as those of the day he had nearly died. Every night he dreamed about what had happened and every dream was a little different from the others. He knew he had left the compound in Muir on foot. He knew he had eaten the sandwiches. He knew he drank the vodka. After that, things got a little fuzzy.

Sometimes he dreamed that he had been carried the two miles to the intersection with the main road in the arms of a huge grizzly bear. He was not sure why he thought that, but he suspected the stink in his lungs, the stink of his own heaving stomach, had somehow reminded him of the smell those big bears had when one encountered them up close and personal in the wild. Or maybe it was just because he could not remember walking and could not imagine how he could've walked after the Cantabuse had kicked in.

Sometimes he dreamed that an eagle had talked to him, urging him, "One more step, just one more step," again and again while a raven countered, "Just give up, Bishop. Just give up. It's too much."

The doctors said hallucinations were not uncommon in his situation, even though his situation was not common enough for them to be able to legitimately discuss its commonalities. It was weird, but wasn't that weird, is what he thought they meant. Or maybe they just were trying to say that they did not have a clue.

It was one of those mysteries that might not be settled this side of Heaven. Bishop was going to add it to the list of things he wanted to ask God when he was called home. The list seemed to get longer all the time. Bishop guessed that must mean he was getting older.

"Are you sleeping?" Diane stood in the doorway wearing traveling blacks. Was this the day that they had agreed she was leaving for Kake? He thought that was next week.

"Your clothes?" He raised his eyebrows. "Tell me your flight is not today."

"No. It's next week. Remember? We discussed it just yesterday." She looked concerned and Bish imagined that she feared one of the long-lasting results of his episode might be some form of dementia or Alzheimer's.

"Those are your traveling blacks?" He doubted himself for a moment.

"Yes. Everything else is at the cleaners." She smiled, understanding his confusion as a justifiable, understandable confusion. He could tell she was relieved.

"So, everything else is in Tucson or already in Kake?" He thought that was right.

"Yes," she smiled. "I may have to go shopping."

"Oh, no." He pretended to be horrified. "I will have to get three more jobs to pay for that."

"No," she smiled. "You will have to get at least four."

They both laughed then. Diane had never been a shopper. One of the biggest challenges of being a mother to two daughters for her had been to understand that her girls like to go hunting for clothes and makeup and shoes even when they did not need any of those things. It was a recreational activity, not a consumer concern.

"We're just going shopping, Mom." Their older daughter, Daphne, used to say. "We're not going shopping shopping."

"Right," Chloe would agree. "We want to go shopping, not buying."

To Diane that seemed silly and pointless, but it made her girls happy, and wasn't that what really mattered after all?

"Four more jobs?" Bish sighed. "I may have to hire an assistant."

"Or a babysitter," Diane frowned.

"All right already. It's great to see you too sweetheart."

"I just worry. That's all. You know that," Diane looked tired.

She stayed and visited for about half an hour, the maximum amount of time allowed by the doctors, and they both tried to keep the conversation light. As is to be expected in any marriage that's lasted over three decades, they'd had their rough times, their ups and downs, peaks and valleys, good times and bad times. They were no strangers to adversity, but still, somehow, this was something new. This was the first time death had been quite so close.

Bishop was surprised that it was affecting them the way it was. How many funerals had he done as a pastor? How many widows had Diane hugged? How many grieving families had they fed and counseled and loved? Obviously, too many to count. Yet, this was different.

Bish could have pretended that it was different because it was them, not somebody else, that it was their family, not some other family. That was part of that. A small part of it. Not the most troubling part for Diane.

The most troubling part for Diane was that Bishop had risked dying in order to prevent returning to being the man he had once been. He had thought she would be better off without him than with him in a diminished or lesser or less controlled capacity. On his part, it had seemed pragmatic.

"You are a stupid son of a bitch when you are drinking," Diane said to him that third week in the hospital when she finally understood his motivation. "You are, however, my stupid son of a bitch. And I love you."

"I love you too," was all he could say.

Love is certainly a strange thing, he told himself, as he drifted off to sleep now. Maybe he should try to dream about love instead of about bears and birds and booze and sandwiches. It was worth a try at least.

Come, quickly, sleep, he prayed. Come quickly.

Chapter 2

She could have done it by herself, Diane assured him when she returned from Kake, but it had been great to have Aunt Posie there to help. Her advice and her town contacts had been great. The hard-weird sisters and their store had been great. They both had great senses of humor, similar but not identical. But both great. Bish began to think his wife was trying for a Guiness record of using the word "great" in one conversation.

The food? Great. Weather? Great. Plane rides? Great. Neighbors? Great. It could get on a fellow's nerves were he a lesser, more impatient man than the Rev. Dr. Bishop Bishop Brewan, Bishop to Southeast Alaska for the Ecumenical Partners in Christ (EPIC) church. Still, it was great to see Diane so happy. Great. Great. Great.

Bish was walking with a cane now. Not for any specific injuries but for a balance problem. The doctors said the problem, a momentary dizziness upon standing up quickly or turning his head too fast, would probably go away. Probably.

Bish was not pleased at first, grumbling about being "enfeebled" but became less upset when Diane told him he should enjoy it.

"Look at it as an excuse to board planes early," she suggested, "and permission to carry a club in public."

"Oh. That could have its advantages." She knew him too well.

"I knew you'd like that."

"Do you know," he pretended to be serious, "are sword canes legal in Alaska?"

"Don't even think about it."

Hearing her automatic response, her quick putdown after so many weeks of measured, carefully calculated answers, was great. She believed he was healing, and hearing that in her voice, he believed it now too. Everything was great, indeed.

The warm Tucson air was great. Seeing their grandchildren at least twice a week was great. And knowing he was going back to work at the end of the month was great too. Or at least both of them were pretending that it was.

Great would be when he began to find answers to all the questions he had pondered for two months now. Greater would be when he discovered who could be trusted and who could not. Greatest would be when he knew whether or not he could trust himself in the field any more, whether his instincts and intuitions, his perceptions and interpretations were still valid and accurate and acute. Did he still have what it took to be Bishop?

At first the Elders had been very cautious. There were so many loose ends. Authorities found the compound devoid of any fingerprints except Bish's. There was no sign of The Teacher. Blue Bandanna Boy had disappeared and so had Pretty Pretty Girl. Aside from the door that he had smashed himself, there was no sign of violence or struggle or of any illegal activities. Except for trespassing and squatting. How could anyone regard Bish's story with less than a tad bit of skepticism?

Disbelief, however, was really not the issue. Evidence was the issue. Without any evidence there was no crime. Without any crime there was no further reason to investigate. Without investigation nothing would ever be discovered. It all seemed so fruitless.

Bish was not sure where to begin, and Jaegar was not much help either. What could he do? He asked the same question now that he asked every day.

"What can I do?" asked the Elder Director, watching Bish's face on the computer screen.

"Well, we have to do something." Bish's voice still trembled. He hated that. It made him sound feeble, old, not quite right.

"Of course. We have to do something. But we do not have to do something yet. Let it rest a while. You know how this works. Sooner or later they will make a mistake."

"Yes, sooner or later they will. But is sooner or later soon enough for Pretty Pretty Girl and Blue Bandanna Boy?" Bish stared at Jaegar's face.

"They do have names, you know?"

"Oh, yes, I know. James Aaron and Trixie Foster. It's just a habit I have. You know that."

Jaegar smiled. "Yes, I know that. Sometimes, however, I want to make sure."

"Make sure of what?" Bishop watched the Elder Director's face carefully.

"Don't make me say it, Bish. You know you almost died. I am responsible to the Elders and to you and to Diane and to your family to always make sure."

"Oh, I know it, brother. I know it, but I don't like it."

"Welcome to adulthood, Bish. And welcome to my world." They both chuckled then.

By the end of the call they agreed that Bish would return to

Kake on a "part-time" basis. The definition of part-time was not clearly defined. Bish would be allowed to pace himself as he felt appropriate. The implied message was not that anyone feared he would not work enough but rather that he would work way too much. This, the Elder Director made very clear, was not to happen. If Bish ended up back in the hospital, his appointment would be over. Someone else would be sent to Southeast Alaska to continue EPIC's work there.

Bish left the on-line meeting unable to fully explain it but fully convinced that if Diane were not going back to the Southeast with him that he would not be going back there either, at least not as an EPIC representative. Posie's Perch, their little Kake cottage, would still be there, and the church would not, could not, ask him to leave it. They would, however, ask him to leave his job, to retire, and to let someone else pursue their missions and investigations.

Bish thought about all the pastors currently in Southeast Alaska. He could imagine none of them taking up his task. That was troublesome. What would've happened early in the Christian movement if Barnabas had not been willing to give Paul a chance? What would've happened if Paul had totally rejected Timothy? He really felt it was the responsibility of each generation to train and prepare the next generation. He had neglected that. Perhaps it was time he found someone to train, to teach, to replace himself? He could not go on forever.

That was one of the big challenges of being a Christian. One did fully intend to go on forever. The "forever" was not in this world, unfortunately. Or not exactly unfortunately. Bish could not imagine living to be 150 or 200 years old. That would be hell. He expected to live forever in eternity with God but sometimes that expectation, that hope, could make one forget about the importance of the here and now. It could lull one into being a poor steward of time in this realm.

Bish leaned on his cane, trying to catch his breath. He really was not ready, but he would be. He would be ready. He had to be ready. Too many people were counting on him. Including God.

Chapter 3

Nobody in the office understood why Briggs was still alive. What had happened to The Boss? No one had ever seen him as angry as he was that day he returned on the helicopter empty-handed. They would have been less surprised to find themselves all dead now, one and a half months later, than they were to discover that Briggs was still alive.

But there he was, standing at the secretary's desk, smiling, looking as if nothing at all was wrong. It made no sense at all. Something was very wrong in their world. It made them afraid, even more afraid than usual.

And then it got worse. The door to The Boss's office opened and The Boss came out smiling. He threw open his arms and Briggs looked at him and grinned.

"Hey, Boss. Thanks for taking the time to see me."

"No problem, Briggs. I'm so glad you stopped by."

Then the two men actually hugged each other. Everyone stared. Was it the end of the world? What was going on? How could this be happening?

"Come on in, Briggs." With his arm around Briggs shoulder,

The Boss guided him into his office and closed the door. Everyone sat breathlessly, waiting for an explosion or a gunshot or some indication of an obscene violence taking place behind that door. But there was nothing. Nothing happened.

The secretary exhaled loudly and a junior junior executive on the far side of the office cleared his throat. All across the room eyes locked for a brief moment and then heads looked down, back down to their desks, back to their paperwork, back to their computers, back to their phones. The world was changing, changing in ways they did not understand, but they still understood they were not changes to be discussed aloud.

Behind that closed-door, in The Boss's office, the two figures sat chuckling now.

"How does it fit?" The Boss tilted his head from side to side looking at Briggs.

"I am still getting used to it. But I think it will work okay." Briggs smiled at The Boss. "It always takes some adjustment."

"Oh," The Boss grand. "You don't have to tell me that, Briggsy baby. You don't have to tell me that. I have lost track of all the times I have had to adjust and readjust."   He sat for a moment thinking about Briggs, remembering his dying screams, the look on his face as he fell from the helicopter, his eyes staring up at The Boss as his body fell down, down, down to the rocks.

"The repairs were fast." It was not a question, but a question was implied. Briggs looked at The Boss closely.

"Oh, yes. They did go quite well. Our guys get better all the time." He smiled at his use of the term "our guys."

"Well, I am glad that they do." Briggs chuckled. "So, what's next?"

"Well, we have to take care of Brewan and Aaron and Foster. Not necessarily in that order, but they have to be priorities right now.

Loose ends are not a good thing. And three loose ends, well, three loose shoestrings could trip anyone up, even us. Right?" His mouth smiled but his eyes did not.

"Yes," the new Briggs nodded his head, his new head, slowly. "Yes, loose ends. Loose ends are not a good thing."

"So let's talk about tying up those problems." The Boss stopped smiling.

The new Briggs nodded. "Yes, let's talk."

"And make some plans."

"Of course, old friend. And make some plans."

A hour and a half later Briggs left the office. Nobody watched him go. Everyone was much too busy to look up. Everyone was working very hard. Everyone was doing exactly what they should be doing. Briggs tried not to smile, looking at all those poker faces. The Boss did not even try. He was laughing out loud when he closed his office door.

Chapter 4

There were only two people in the caves who remembered Blue Bandanna Boy from before. Of course they did not call him Blue Bandanna Boy. They called him Jimmy. He had been Jimmy, little Jimmy, the last time they had seen him, but he was not little now, nor did Jimmy seem like quite the right name.

He had arrived in the middle of the night, walking in the darkness, the short Alaska summer darkness, through the rocks that led to the cave's entrance. He had ignored the challenge at the mouth of cage, walking right past the older man who said "Stop" three times in the best scary voice he could muster. But Jimmy had not even slowed down.

Now he sat behind the fire, leaning against the cave wall, drinking coffee from a cup he had taken from a tub of dishes, taken without even asking permission, taken without being reprimanded, just taken. The two who had known him before both wondered if his eyes had always looked this way.

"How's it going, Jimmy?" The older of the two men spoke.

"Where have you been, Jimmy?" the younger added his voice.

"The name is Muck."

"Muck?" The younger man of the two started to laugh but a warning look from the older stopped him. There was something wrong with those eyes. It was better to be careful.

"It's good to meet you, Muck. Welcome to our little family."

Muck looked at the two of them and nodded slowly. "Thank you, gentlemen. It's good to meet you too."

Everyone else just watched. The three teenage girls watched. The two adolescent boys watched. The tired looking middle-aged woman and her husband both watched. Even the small child playing too close to the fire watched. They all knew this was an important time.

"I won't be staying long," Muck watched them now. "Not more than two days. I appreciate your hospitality."

Two days? Apparently he understood, understood the rules of the cave. "After three days fish and visitors stink." But he was only staying two. He was not a threat, even though he looked very much like he might be. No one bothered him while he slept leaning against the cave wall.

People had been living in the Sitka caves for at least a century before the Edgecombe Disaster. Homeless folks, battered wives, addicts and alcoholics, runaway teens, and people fleeing from the law all found shelter there over the years. Most of the time they were transients, arriving and departing before those chasing them or seeking them could catch up. Most of the time they avoided long-lasting relationships or commitments, believing or at least pretending to believe this was all temporary. Most of the time they would return again and again to the caves because they would make the same stupid mistakes again and again or because other people in their lives made the same stupid mistakes with them or for them again and again.

Sometimes there was a sense of community, but the concept of family, the kind of family the two men who knew Muck talked about, seldom survived here. There were too many histories, too many memories, too many stories of families gone wrong to ever let the idea of family live long. Most folks who came to the caves did not want to belong, did not want to be friends, did not even want to believe long-term relationships were possible for them. They just wanted to be left alone.

Traditionally, the people of Sitka had followed a live and let live policy with the cave people. After all, it was Alaska, and you never knew when your own circumstances might change. One bad fishing season could cost you your boat and your home. One plane crash could destroy your family and your future. A tsunami could turn your world upside down and wash your life out to sea. You might become a cave dweller yourself without any warning or notice. It was best not to judge too quickly or too soon or too much at all.

Organizations in the town did what they could to help. Churches offered free weekly dinners. Food pantries and co-ops provided canned goods and fresh vegetables in season. The fire department offered first aid courses and the hospital did free screenings.

There was always, however, courteous caution involved. Many of the townspeople were descendants of fiercely independent Alaskans, Native and non-Native. They understood what it meant to be self-reliant, what it meant to be independent, what it meant to be left alone, and they were careful not to interfere under the guise of helping. They were careful to let people sort out who they were and what they wanted to be on their own, if that's what they wanted. Many of their parents and grandparents had come to Alaska to escape situations and circumstances in other parts of the world. Many of their families understood that need to "start over" and they would do nothing to rob others of that opportunity, if that's what they wanted.

This independent ethic, combined with the Alaskan Native traditions of sustenance living and communal winter homes, had made the caves "safe" places, dangerous but safe places for decades before the Edgecombe Disaster. After that, the sustainability of the tradition and the place was questionable, just like the rest of the planet. After the Edgecomb Disaster, after The Melt began, the whole concept of "afterness" and especially a "happily ever after"ness, became alien. Few believed they could count on anything now.

Blue Bandanna Boy, Muck now, still seemed to be sleeping, but he was not. He was listening. He was listening to the voices in the cave and the voices in his head, trying to sort out what had happened and what was happening and what might happen from what he hoped would happen. It was giving him a headache.

The Teacher's directions had been less than helpful. "Scatter, disappear, and wait." That was it? That was it. Not very helpful, not very helpful at all.

Muck knew that some of Teacher's followers listened to everything he said. They had saved money and hidden supplies and arranged safe places to stay. They could disappear for a while, playing refugee and fugitive with their families and families of their friends. They could keep their heads down and pretend to be normal and do everything one needed to do and do nothing one needed not to do to draw attention to themselves. They were poseurs. He suppressed a laugh. Teacher would not expect him to know that word. But he did. And sometimes he thought Teacher was a poseur too.

For so long he had been afraid of The Teacher, afraid of his power and his connections, afraid of what he knew and what he could do, but now, as his own powers grew and his own understanding increased, he had begun to think The Teacher was just a tool. A tool in all the senses of the word.

Muck was beginning to understand. There were two choices in life--you could be a user or you could be used. If you were not a mechanic, you were a tool. And he was tired of being a tool. It was time to be a mechanic, to be an engineer, to be in control. In control of his life, and the lives of others. It was time to say goodbye to Jimmy and hello to Muck.

Chapter 5

Trixie Foster, aka Pretty Pretty Girl, was devastated. It was happening again. She tried to pretend that it was not, but something deep inside her told her that it was. She had been used and abused and dumped again. Teacher had been like all the others.

Oh, he was pretending that things were different. He had told them all to scatter and had counseled for patience and perseverance. He told them to wait. Teacher had made promises but she knew he would never keep those promises. It was happening again. Was she never going to learn? How stupid could she be?

Briefly, she had considered being very stupid, considered ending it all. How hard could it be? A quick jump off the ferry? A casual late-night stroll into bear country? A quick squeeze of the trigger and a brief blinding headache? She had considered it briefly.

But she was not the stupid stupid girl that they all thought she was. Why should she make it easy for them? Why should their faithlessness and their meanness be her problem? Why should she let them determine who and what she was? And where were these thoughts coming from? Where had she heard them before?

She sat and thought about it. She had been riding the ferries for a week now, having outstayed her welcome with old acquaintances who had never really been friends. No one seemed to have noticed so far. As long as she bought the tickets with cash money and kept to herself she was doing okay. She might manage another week on the boats. But she knew that she was pretty. Teacher had been right about that. Sooner or later someone would notice and she would have to run again.

It seemed like she had been running her entire life. Always running away. Never running to. Always making do. Never striving to. And she was tired. She was too tired to even think straight now. What had she been asking? Oh, yes. These new thoughts. What was their source?

It was too hard to think, even though it seemed to be suddenly very necessary. She needed to rest. She needed a place to rest and hide until she could understand these thoughts. She needed some place safe, some place where she could be Trixie Foster, not just the stupid stupid blonde girl.

And then she thought of Veronica. Ronni was a blonde girl too, but no one seemed to think that she was stupid. No one seemed to boss her around. No one wanted to hurt her. Maybe she should not have run so readily away from that place where people might have been doing more than just pretending to care?

In the safety of the bathroom stall she counted her money. She had enough and it was worth a try, wasn't it? Well, she was worth the try. She really was, and so she would.

She thought she had it all figured out, or at least had figured out a place where she could figure out the rest. She could hide there and rest there and maybe be safe there for a while, if they did not turn out to be assholes like the rest of the world. And when they did, at least she would have eaten well and slept in a safe warm bed, probably. And the rest? Whatever the rest was she would unravel one day at a time.

She thought she had it all figured out, but when she stood on the porch in the dim glow of the Sheldon twilight and knocked and Ronni opened the door and wrapped her arms around her and they both stood and cried and cried, she was not so sure anymore. But that was okay too.

Chapter 6

Bishop Bishop was getting tired of Diane's stories. Why had Posie left all those journals behind? And why did his wife find them so fascinating? He sighed. Because Diane was Diane. That was reason enough.

"That was a deep sigh. Are you alright?" She watched him like a hawk these days. That was a saying from his Pennsylvania grandmother too. Maybe he should say "watched him like an eagle" now that they were back here in Kake?

"Finer than frog hair." Another Penn's Woods expression?

"Okay. Shall I continue or am I boring you?"

"Diane Brewan, you could never do less than fascinate me."

"But these stories are boring you? Just a bit?"

"Only because I know most of them too well."

"Then let's take a walk, Bish. I'll grab your cane."

Unless he had to stand too long, or unless the floors were concrete, or he walked too long uphill, or downhill, Bish did not need the cane now. Around the cottage they had christened Posie's Perch in honor of his aunt, he was fine. On ferries and planes and in the truck Uncle Martin had left for them when he and Posie moved south, he was fine. Standing behind the pulpit when he filled in for the pastors of EPIC's Southeast Alaska churches, he was fine. The Rev. Dr. Bishop Brewan, Bishop of the Ecumenical Partners in Christ Church, was fine.

Except that he was tired all the time. Too tired too often, at least, to be happy with his recovery. He sighed again.

"I don't know where I left it. My cane."

"I do."

He tried not to think of it as therapy, but it was, this walking Diane wanted him to do every day. It was therapy. Therapy was for old people and he wasn't old. Not quite yet.

He had decided when he turned fifty that he wasn't going to be old, become old, before he turned eighty, at least. He would be one of those "spry old guys" that Aunt Posie referred to in her journals, townspeople who lived longer and acted younger than anyone could have ever expected. That plan had seemed easier then than it did now. Oh, well. It was still a goal.

"Stop sighing like that, Bishop Brewan, or I am going to hit you with your own cane." Diane was glaring at him with exasperation.

He laughed. "Sorry. I guess I am glad I didn't find a sword cane after all."

They both laughed then and the walk was better today than yesterday's. And yesterday's had been better than any of last week's. He was mending, was healing, just not as fast as he wanted to. Aunt Posie was right. Getting old was not for sissies.

The walk was better because he was getting better, but it was better also because today there was no rain in Kake, Alaska. Not yet. Rain would come. Rain always came.

Sometimes Bish understood the practices the New Noahs had

taken in the last decade. In some parts of the world, building an ark might not be the worst response one could muster for the worsening weather. There were places where it did seem to rain all the time. Once Ketchikan had been the Tongass Rain Forest town in Southeast Alaska claiming the most ridiculous annual rainfall, but now as its number pushed two hundred inches annually and the rest of the panhandle rushed to catch up, it wasn't amusing or quaint or entertaining anymore. Scary and depressing were more like it.

If it wasn't for the long days of summer when the sun shone even during many of the rain storms, shone dimly through the mist for the most part, but that was better than no sun, Kake might become a very depressing place to live. Bish shook his head at that thought. Already Alaska had a suicide rate over five times that of the Lower 48. And it had been worse before The Melt, before so many cities and lives had been wrecked and so many had lost the will to live. Alaska's numbers had not gone down; the rest of the country's had risen.

Kake might be depressing for visitors if they stayed too long, if they tried to survive the long dark wet winters when the sun disappeared for eighteen hours a day, at least. Kake might be depressing for anyone who didn't have a focus, a purpose, a goal, a reason for living, but wasn't that true anywhere? What was life without purpose, without a cause and a call? Even in the sunniest places people gave up and gave in and cashed in their chips when they had no reason to live.

Wow, Bish, he caught himself. Are you trying to depress yourself? You have a nice home here. Diane is here. You still have your job, your call, and challenges galore. You did not fall back into drinking when it would have been easy to do so. God has blessed you in too many ways to count. Get a grip.

Bish gripped his cane and spun it around his fingers, raising his arm up and down, letting the polished wooden stick roll across his neck and down into left hand, and then flipped it back to his right. He smiled as Diane stopped walking and stared at him.

"What was that?"

"What was what?" He knew he had a sheepish grin on his face, but he couldn't help it.

"That move with the cane? Are you going Kung Fu Bishop on me?"

"Maybe." He raised one leg and both arms, holding them in a bent elbow, bent wrists position popular in old vids sometimes shown at the community center.

"Really?"

"Or maybe I just knew the moves from when our younger daughter was on flag line in high school?"

"Maybe you are just a nut."

He smiled. "Maybe that too." He smiled because they both knew that even if he was a nut, he was her nut, and she was his, and that was all that mattered.

The rain began softly, but they knew it would increase. They turned back to Posie's Perch, hastening along the street nearest the bay's waters, passing the old church submerged beneath the bay, imagining they could see the glimmer of the Head Start building submerged beside it and the old elementary school in front, its red siding turning brown in the waves and silt slapping against it year after year.

They climbed three blocks up the steep cross street and hastened down their lane past the fire department and police station, faster than Bish liked, but he didn't tell Diane. The rain hit hard as they crossed the new deck that had welcomed Bish when he had returned with Diane after their stay in Tucson with the kids, a gift from the kids and Martin and Posie, an addition Bish and Diane had talked about but had figured they couldn't afford for a few years. It was for Christmas and birthdays and anniversaries and whatevers for the next five years the family told them. And it was much appreciated.

Inside now, sitting in front of the glass doors that opened onto the deck, they sipped blucaf, a warm calming cup of comfort that tasted of blueberries and caffeine and just a touch of chocolate. Those Kagi folks got better all the time, thought Bish.

Diane asked about lunch and Bish said, "Maybe later," and they both fell asleep in their chairs, watching the rain, listening to the water, glad to be together.

Chapter 7

In California people would have loved to have even a quarter of the rain falling in Kake. In the last decade the place had become so desert-like that millions had moved away, some to Colorado and Oregon and Utah and many to Alaska. Wine country was a thing of the past and the new tech center of the nation was Des Moines, another suggestion for a new national capital from lawmakers tired of the mosquitos and swamps of a sinking District of Columbia.

The fabulous film industry was a thing of the past too, at least in California. Toronto was the place to be now, if you wanted to produce or star in films. The huge increase in Great Lakes shipping and the climate warmed by The Melt made the Canadian city attractive to artists of all sorts. The advent of the Ameca, the American, Mexican, Canadian dollar modeled after the Euro, simplified trade too.

California had not fallen into the ocean as alarmists of earlier centuries had predicted it would when the San Andreas attacked, but The Melt and all its effects had certainly sent its economy down the drain. Nobody dreamed of moving there anymore. Children were growing up talking of Toronto and Texas, dreaming of lives in Alaska and Australia, but California? No thanks.

The Teacher understood. He'd spent nearly a quarter of a year in that wreck of a state and he felt like a prune left out in the sun too long. The backs of his hands looked like an old man's and he couldn't keep enough sunscreen on his face and neck. What a dump. Maybe Dante should add a circle called California to his depiction of Hell.

Randolph had driven to Bellingham in the old Chevy owned by the girl he'd charmed and lived with for those three months of hiding and waiting. She didn't need cars any more. It was not very powerful or attractive, sort of like she had been, he chuckled, but it had a good air conditioner.

Bellingham, Washington was still the best place in the Lower 48 to hop on the Alaska Marine Highway System and travel up the coast to Southeast Alaska. Randolph had considered taking the car along, fairly certain no one would bother to look for it even if they ever found the girl's remains out there in the blowing sands, but the voices had counseled against it and he had listened. Local law enforcement was overworked to the point of exhaustion and extinction in California, and the feds wouldn't waste too much time investigating the disappearance of a junkie girl with no family or friends even if they somehow became involved, The Teacher felt safe, but why bother with the car? He could get one back in the panhandle if he needed to.

His people had always been resourceful, living off the land and the sea and all they provided. He could live off all the strangers and invaders the land and sea attracted now. He was going home.

Not back to Kake or to Muir, of course. And not to Sheldon. Ketchikan was too far south and Juneau was too busy. He needed a place on the ferry route but not so much so that he might accidentally run into his annoying cousin and his stupid friends. Where would Bishop probably never visit? Probably Sitka.

Probably Sitka where Bishop's parents had died in the Edgecombe Disaster when the mountain had spewn fire and lava and ash suddenly and violently. Probably Sitka where the remains of the old university decayed, allowing the signs of the Christian invaders to sink into the wet ground of the muskeg. Probably Sitka where he knew no one and nobody knew him. At least not yet.

Good idea, the voices affirmed. Sitka was sound. Sitka was smart. Sitka had potential. In Sitka we can plan for the future and recapture the past. Set sail for Sitka.

The Teacher smiled. The voices had not wasted his time in California. He had been hiding but he had been studying too. Once California had been home to one of the finest educational systems in the world. Still, its neglected libraries and learning centers held stories and histories he could access and use. He had learned so much more about how power and powers operated.

Things would be different this time. Posie and Martin had settled in the South. Stupid Cousin Bish didn't have their extensive Kake connections and history. He wouldn't know who to distrust. He would feel safe and think Kake was a sanctuary, a place of respite from the travails of his travels and encounters.

How wrong he would be. And how devastated EPIC would be when it all fell apart. There were different ways to fight a war. An enemy could be attacked or an enemy could be persuaded that there was nothing to attack. When foes pretend to be friends, when enmity masquerades as amity, motivation for confrontation evaporates.

EPIC would be defeated not by opposition but by assimilation. First, cooperation. Then, duplication. And finally, delegation. It had worked before in too many other places to count. It would work in The Teacher's home too. "Let's work together on common goals" would become "Let's not waste resources by duplicating services" and then morph into "You are needed elsewhere more. We can handle this now without you."

The Teacher smiled. "They never really learn," he whispered to himself. "They never really learn."

Chapter 8

Ronni and Van shared the belief that addictions never go away, are never really cured, can never be regarded as resolved or as part of the past. They had known people with alcohol addictions, drug addictions, sex addictions, smoking addictions, eating addictions, internet addictions, control addictions, and vocation and avocation addictions. There did not appear to be anything in the world that could not become an addiction for someone somewhere given the right wrong circumstances. They had no trouble now agreeing that their young blonde guest had a compensation addiction.

Trixie Foster, privately they called her "Tricksy," was addicted to compensating for the lack of love and affection and approval in her childhood by any means she could muster and master. She wanted desperately to be wanted and needed excessively to be needed. The want and the need were not what made the addiction. They were part of being human. It was the desperation and the excessiveness that brought in the addiction qualities.

Ivan knew that he was luckier in his own addiction than were many addicts. He could just not drink alcohol. It wasn't easy and he did still take a drug that would make him very ill if he did drink, but he could avoid alcohol. How could an overeater avoid food? People have to eat. And how could Trixie avoid love?

"We all want to be loved," he frowned at his wife. "It's part of human nature."

"I know," Ronni frowned right back at him. "You can avoid the bars and I can stay away from other junkies, but how can a sex addict avoid human's bodies or a control freak avoid people in power?"

"You know what Bish would say, don't you?"

"That sin is part of human nature too, that it can't be avoided."

Van nodded. "Right. If we were capable of sinlessness on our own, Jesus would not have needed to die for us."

"That's not what some religions teach," Ronni looked straight into his eyes.

Van returned her stare, "And that's why they are wrong."

"Get a room, you too," Trixie stared at them across the dinner table. "Or change the subject. You are making me very uncomfortable here."

"Deal with it," Ronni grinned at her. "And eat your carrots."

"Yes, Mom," Trixie did a dead-on imitation of an exasperated teen girl's sigh.

"And none of that 'Mom' stuff either. I am young enough to be your sister."

"Okay, Sis. Sorry." She pretended remorse as she stuffed a forkful of carrots into her mouth.

Ronni heard the test. Trixie had called her "Sis" and had waited to be challenged or corrected. She would use the appellation again soon repeatedly and watch to see if the implied relationship was accepted or rejected.

Van's raised right eyebrow told her he'd heard it too. They were both wondering if it was an attempt to gain acceptance or to gain control. With a girl as misused and rejected as "Tricksy" it could be an effort to find family or a ploy to create capital to be cashed in later.

She had done both repeatedly over the past weeks. They hoped they had caught her at it most of the time.

"Ronni, come in here right now," Van had called to his wife in the kitchen the second day of Trixie's stay with them when the little blonde had wandered into their bedroom wearing only a towel around her body still dripping from the shower and asked Van where they kept their hair dryer.

"Oh, no. There will none of that." Ronni had appeared instantly. "Get your wet shiny butt and boobs out of here and get dressed for breakfast."

"I just wanted the hairdryer."

"Move it now or you won't have any hair to dry when I'm done with you."

Van grinned after she left. "Thanks, Hon."

"We knew that would happen. The kid is kinda cute too."

"I didn't notice."

"Good answer, Husband."

"Thank-you, Wife." Van knew Ronni would have a follow-up discussion with the little blonde later when he was not around. And he was glad he wouldn't be around.

There had been the expected money stealing incident. A twenty Ameca bill Van left on the dining room table for Ronni to give the boy who delivered groceries disappeared the fourth day Trixie was in the house. That night at dinner Ronni set two plates of food on the table, one for Van and one for herself. When Van looked questioningly at her she just shrugged.

"We ran out of food money."

"Ran out? How?"

"It just disappeared, Van."

"How weird is that?"

Trixie said nothing, sitting silently while they ate and discussed their busy days and planned their schedules for the next. No one made any accusations or explanations, but Van after that left money on the table frequently and no more disappeared.

Of course, the normal childish game of pitting one partner against the other was attempted, asking Van after Ronni said "No" and vice versa. It didn't work. Staying out after curfew resulted in being locked out all night, sleeping in the garage. Clothes and belongings tossed on the floor of her room like trash instead of being put away somehow ended up in the trash. Refusal to attend AA meetings meant being locked out of the house, including the garage, until the couple returned. They were still waiting for her to bring a man home or to try to steal the car.

Surprisingly, she hadn't stolen anything from the house to hock at the little pawn shop in town and she had gone to church with them every Sunday. Pastor Patrick Murphy's wife kept an eagle eye on her there after she gushed over the sermon to Rev. Murphy following the service her first week. Mrs. Murphy knew trouble when she saw it.

Van and Ronni tried not to laugh.

Gradually, Trixie began to seek positive affirmation more than just existence affirmation, but the Jacksons knew it would be a lengthy trip down a long road filled with potholes and roadblocks for "Tricksy." There were so many things to learn, and so many to unlearn, before she would be able to discover herself as a creature made in God's image and loved and valued by Him. After that, she might learn to love and value herself and others too.

Once, when asked by a neighboring couple if they were going to "start a family someday," Van had responded in joking manner that was an attempt to discourage that line of questioning,

"We've thought about waiting until we're in our sixties and then adopting a thirty year old couple and inviting them to Sunday dinner once a month. It sounds cheaper and less heartbreaking than how most do the parent thing."

With Tricksy in the house the idea seemed rather a good one after all. It had seemed so calm and peaceful before. She wasn't noisy or clumsy or anything else that earned her the label "under foot," but she seemed that way more than a few times as the weeks passed.

Chapter 9

Elder Director Jacob Jaegar did not like getting phone calls from or about Rev. Dr. Bishop Brewan. Receiving calls from Mrs. Diane Brewan was even worse. Bish would at least pretend to agree and give in when he and the Elder Director disagreed over policies and practices and procedures, and then he would do things his way regardless. Mrs. Brewan would not even pretend.

Now she was trying to convince Jaegar that her husband needed to be allowed to start making his Bishop's rounds again, "For the safety and sanity of all involved."

Jaegar did not tell her that Pastor Molly from Kake had already called him today and gently made the same suggestion. Or request. Apparently, Bish was using some of his extra time in Kake to be an "extra set of hands" in Molly's ministries, and she was getting tired of his looking over her shoulder and second guessing her methods and goals.

Like too many suddenly retired husbands and pastors, Bish was getting in the way of others' calls and careers. Jaegar remembered how his own mother, a high-school music teacher, had answered him when he'd asked how she and his father, a city planner, were doing six months after they both retired.

"Having your father at home is like having a piano in the kitchen, Jake. Sometimes we make beautiful music together, but most of the time he's just in the way."

Apparently, Diane Brewan was tired of the music now too and wanted her kitchen back, metaphorically. And probably physically too. Jaegar knew the bishop had developed some strange culinary tastes when he was on his own, before Diane had moved to the panhandle. He remembered Pastor Patrick Murphy from Sheldon telling him he'd received a certificate from a Tlingfrench restaurant for his birthday. What was that anyway? Salmon stuffed with snails? Or maybe crusty bread with seaweed? Jaegar didn't think he really wanted to know.

"Have Bish call me, Diane, and we'll discuss him returning to the field full-time."

"I'll have him call tomorrow. But we never had this conversation. Understand?"

"I understand." And sometimes he regretted that he'd never married? Craziness.

Chapter 10

Four months after he'd nearly died, nearly killed himself Diane would have corrected him, the Rev. Dr. Bishop Brewan, EPIC Bishop to Southeast Alaska was back in Muir, Alaska celebrating communion with the tiniest, newest church congregation in his charge. It felt good.

Brian Meade was the oldest EPIC pastor in the Southeast but one of the least experienced. He'd started his working career as a chef in Cleveland, Ohio, so he knew all the answers to Bish's questions about Angloamish cuisine. On EPIC policy and polity, he was not as sharp.

"Stuffed woodchuck with dandelion greens?"

"Cooked it. Served it. Hated it." Brian liked to talk in short sentences, chopping his words into brief ideas the way he chopped meat in the kitchen. Quickly. Efficiently. Almost brutally.

Bish laughed. "You or the customers? Hated it?"

"Me. They loved it."

"Baby redskin potatoes and fresh trout cooked in apple cider?"

"An abomination. It insults all the ingredients." Meade

shuddered.

Bishop could not imagine anyone getting to know Brian Meade would dislike him. He was forthright to a fault and blunter than he'd ever let his kitchen knives be, but his big heart and his love for the Lord floated around him like an aura. It was invisible but palpable.

"So bring me up to speed on the baptism problem you're having with parents in your congregation, Brian. I'm a little confused."

"Me too. A bit. Dedication versus baptism. That's the issue. I can't find dedication in the book."

"That's because it's not there. EPIC does adult baptism for folks over twelve and infant baptism for children whose parents request it. Folks baptized as children can request an affirmation of baptismal vows later in life, if they want to confirm and accept as their own the promises and commitments their parents made for them as babies."

"So, 'Once forever'?"

"No one is baptized twice. The Holy Spirit doesn't need to be reinstalled or reactivated. But sometimes folks do need or feel the need to recommit themselves."

"Any chance you could explain that? During communion today?" Meade looked dubiously hopeful.

"I'd be glad to, Brian." It was good to be needed again.

The sacraments of the church had been one of the biggest challenges in the formation of the Ecumenical Partners in Christ Church. Some of the merging denominations had six sacraments. Others had only two.

What exactly made a sacrament a sacrament? Did it have to have precedent in the ministries of Jesus himself or was early church tradition enough? Did it require a written record of vocal affirmation from the Christ or did the procedures of his first disciples qualify as normative?

EPIC had settled on three sacraments: baptism, communion, and the blessing of marriage. Believers and the children of believers were baptized. Professing followers of the Christ could partake of the Eucharist. EPIC pastors blessed civil unions that met biblical standards, but they did not perform or officiate at weddings as agents of the state.

Bishop assisted Pastor Meade in the worship service in full regalia. He could tell some of the parishioners were troubled by his appearance while others seemed pleased by it. Many of the younger attendees were used to Pastor Brian's black chef's shirt and white bandana he'd made his regular Sunday look. The Tlingit members, however, and the older folk recognized elements of their childhood spiritual leaders and elders echoed in Bish's black robe with crimson stripes. The red clerical collar he seldom wore proclaimed the specialness of the day, his own office and calling, and his recognition that these few gathered here were his people as much and as importantly as any of the folks in the big churches of Juneau or Ketchikan.

"Success is not about who you are and what you achieve," he finished his brief homily. "Success is about knowing who died for you on that cross so many years ago and about striving to serve him. It's always about choice. Christ calls and we choose. We choose to respond or we choose to ignore. We choose to trust and obey or we choose to turn away. God rejects none who accept Jesus. God accepts none who reject His Son. Amen."

Chapter 11

After a tureen luncheon, "One of the unofficial 'true marks of the true Church,'" Bish joked, Brian Meade drove Bish back to the scene of his "near death experience." Coming down the wet gravel road to the scattering of boulders where he had swallowed the vodka that activated the Cantabuse in his body that nearly killed him, Brewan was disappointed how plain and drab the setting looked. He had hoped for an obviously dramatic scene with boulders higher than houses and torn earth and shattered plants, a setting still reeling from the violence he had experienced there. Lacking that, he would have settled for an inner drama, a moviesque flashback showing forgotten faces and revealing hidden secrets essential to a startling revelation and exciting final plot twist.

How human he was, he smiled to himself. People always want to believe that the world is as affected or altered or devastated as they are by the savages and ravages tearing at them. When we suffer, we expect our neighbors and friends and family and the whole world to suffer too. And we resent it when they do not. When a loved one dies, we can't understand how the sun still rises and we marvel at the birds still singing in the trees and the clouds still winging across the skies. As we lower a friend killed at sea into the earth that is their final berth this side of Heaven, we want to scream at the waves to stop on the water and the wind to be still. We want all the world to feel our suffering when we suffer. We are so selfish and so self-centered.

Yet, we still want to act with impunity and without consequences. We polluted the air forever and dug up and burned the past, but refused to believe our pillaging of the planet hurt it. We wanted it to be too tough to be hurt by us. Bish smiled and shook his head. We always want it both ways. Aunt Posie used to say, "We want to have our cake and eat it too."

"What? Are you okay, Bishop?"

"Are any of us ever really okay, Pastor?"

"I'm not sure what the question is."

"Then the answer would be even more confusing," Bish smiled as he climbed out of the battered white pickup Brian had borrowed from a parishioner.

Returning to the scene of the crime, Bish silently said to himself. But what crime and whose crime exactly? Had he been violated or had he been the perpetrator? Had outside or inside forces clashed here? Where were battles between light and darkness really waged? Was the war on the soil or in the soul?

What a great title for a lecture, or maybe even a whole semester course, "On the Soil or in the Soul?" Always at least partly a pedagogue, aren't you, Bish? He couldn't help it, no matter how much he tried, and usually he saw no reason to try. Why shouldn't others find his life as fascinating and as educational as he did?

He walked around among the large rocks for ten minutes more, hoping a bird would wing its way down from the sky and land there, ominously or protectively, but none did. He watched the hillside for a dark spot to move and reveal itself a looming grizzly, but none did. The landscape was a blank canvas with no artist to bring it to life.

Bish rode back into Muir, asking Brian Meade all the questions a good bishop would ask, murmuring all the clichés of comfort and words of wisdom that were expected from one assigned to be a pastor to the pastors, but he didn't really hear any of the short vague responses Brian offered, and he wouldn't remember much later about the day besides the former cook's look of relief when he declined his offer to go home for dinner with him and spend the night with Meade's family before flying down to Sheldon. Bish was hunting now and he didn't want to lose the trail.

Friar William of Ockham was right so many centuries ago. All things else being equal, the simplest solution to a mystery was the best. Or most likely. Or whatever. One answer seemed obvious, but maybe because he feared it was or wanted it to be? Or both. Anyway, he had to keep looking, Bish told himself, until he found it. Or until he died trying. Now, he just needed to define "it" a tad more. Was it the trail or the trail's end or both? Or The One he'd find there?

Chapter 12

"And you didn't bother to tell me she was here?" Bishop Brewan was furious. "Over two months, no, more like three, and you never said a word?"

Ronni was not going to be intimidated. "No, and if you'd stayed home I wouldn't have told you for another month. Or more if I knew you'd react like this."

"Oh, you knew it. You just wanted to put it off, love," Van interrupted their quarrel in his easy going warm voice that belied the ice in his eyes. "You two are too much alike to pretend either would've acted differently had the roles been reversed." His tone said he'd believe nothing else.

Brewan had arrived at Veronica's home and business to find Beatrice Foster, aka Trixie, aka Tricksy, aka Pretty Pretty Girl working the cash register at the thrift shop counter. Ronni had given her the job, commission only, no salary, and set her loose upon the unsuspecting Sheldonians. Sheldonites? Sheldoners? Bish wasn't sure, but the fact he was wondering meant he was calming down.

"We wanted you to heal, in lots of ways, before you jumped back into the ring, friend," Van smiled again. "We don't want to lose you just quite yet."

"I understand and appreciate that," Bish took a deep breath, "but…"

"No buts. Just understand it and appreciate it. And move on, Bish." Van's voice was less warm now.

He was right too. "I'm sorry, Ronni. Forgive my tantrum."

"Already forgotten. Now let me tell you what we've learned while you've been playing crippled old man." Her smile said it was forgiven. And almost forgotten. Almost.

Bea, apparently the shop's customers had taken to calling her Bea or Bee, didn't know much about the man she called Teacher. Except that he was a jerk. Like most men. She'd made that clear to Ronni repeatedly.

He was Native. Old, but Bee thought anyone over forty outlandishly old, "not as sly as he thinks he is," and "pretty good in the sack," for an old man. And a jerk.

"Not very helpful." Bish resisted commenting that it didn't seem like three months' work, because he knew better. Ronni and Van loved him and would do anything for him, but Tricksy, as they kept calling her, needed them and their love much more than he did. He had them and Diane and the gals, and Martin and Posie. And even Jaegar. Pretty Pretty Girl had them. Period.

And he had to stop thinking of her as Pretty Pretty Girl. Diane's words from their Tucson conversations about the young woman floated to the front of his brain.

"Calling her 'Pretty Pretty Girl' objectifies her, and men have probably done that to her all of her life. People look like they look. You'd never call anyone 'Ugly Ugly Girl.'"

Bish snorted, "Of course not."

"Saying 'Pretty Pretty Girl' is just as offensive. It just pretends to be better. Ask one of our daughters if you don't believe me." Diane smiled at his face.

"Oh, no. I know better than that. Which means I know better period, doesn't it? You are a witch, aren't you? Messing with my mind again."

"Never. And not a 'Weird Sister' or a 'hard-weird' one either."

"Pretty soon you'll tell me saying 'Blue Bandana Boy' is wrong too?"

"Pretty soon. When you're well enough to hear it."

Ronni's cough brought him back to the now. She was expecting a response. Had she asked him a question.

"So, Bee," he tried the new name on his tongue and it seemed okay, "Bee needs us right now a lot more than we need her?" Summarizing, repeating, paraphrasing were always safe ploys.

"Exactly. I knew you'd understand." Ronni filled all their cups with blucaf. This one had a slight tinge of lemon. Bish wasn't sure how much he disliked it. It left a bitter aftertaste in his mouth.

He'd told Diane about his cousin Randolph, but no one else. Partly because he wasn't sure what there was to tell. Partly because his saying it too many times would make it too real. Partly because he couldn't prove all of it.

Later, he would regret not telling Ronni and Van, later but not now. Now they had enough to think about. Care about. Worry about. He could deal with The Teacher for now and they could work with Bee. Sure, Bee sounded okay. He could remember that.

If he was right, and the other choice was that his brain and memory had been affected even more by nearly dying than even his fearful wife and careful doctors thought, The Teacher could be his own cousin Randolph. Probably was, in fact. Occam again. It did run in the family. Sort of.

Uncle Martin's brother Paul had died at sea when his only son, Randolph, was not quite six years old. Bish had assumed for a long time that it was a fishing accident like all the other accidents that had claimed Tlingit and Anglo fisherfolk for centuries in the Southeast. Every family had tales of relatives who went out fishing and never came back, of boats that disappeared and were never found, tales of grief and disaster that were horribly common and individually devastating. No one talked much about Paul. His wife, Sandra, had remarried a few years after the tragedy and created another. Randolph's stepfather was an abusive drunk who drove Ran from home and into the army when he was eighteen.

Service in the nation's armed forces was a long-honored tradition among the Tlingit people, and Ran had been, maybe for the first time, proud to be a part of a family that did not seem entirely dysfunctional. Unlike most young men from the Southeast, he re-upped when his first enlistment was over, and then he did it again, and again. In the end he stayed the full twenty years required for retirement.

God's timing is always the best, Bishop reminded himself now, and it had certainly seemed to be good for Ran. The obscenely inadequate educational opportunities and long-term veterans' benefits system that had been a disgrace to the nation in the last half of the previous century had been remedied at about the time Ran had begun his service. Now soldiers received one year of college education for every year they served, and free health care for life after serving a minimum of ten years. Ran had chosen to study both during and after his time of service, finishing a bachelor's degree in education and a master's in psychology and philosophy by the time he was forty and mustering out. Everyone expected him to finish his education and become a college professor in Juneau or Anchorage. Nobody figured he'd return to Kake.

He hadn't stayed long either. Bish had never been certain why, but had suspected it was the result of some sort of dispute or disagreement with Posie and Martin. He'd never asked and they had been too private to volunteer any information. Bish wondered now if there might be anything enlightening on the subject in Aunt Posie's journals. Perhaps a little research would be a distracting task for Diane? He called her that evening after returning to the room Ronni and Van always saved for him behind their crazy patchwork home.

"Early American Add-a-Shack" was what Van called the architectural style of the house. "Any time we need more space, we add a shack to the one we added before."

"And later," Ronni laughed, "we will add one to it. And on it goes."

Bishop looked out the window into the dying light, remembering the last time he'd slept here, the night he thought he saw a grizzly lumbering into the shadows descending on the little town named for one of his ancestors in the faith. It seemed like years ago instead of just a few months. Time was a strange creature.

As a boy, he'd heard someone, he wasn't sure who it had been, remark that God had created time because people would not be able to handle life if everything happened at once. The older he grew, though, the more it seemed to Bishop Bishop that time was accelerating constantly, constantly jamming one event after another in increasingly rapid succession, so that life was a blur so much of the time. Years now were shorter than summers had been when he was a boy playing on his Pennsylvania grandparent's farm. Decades passed more quickly than fishing trips with Uncle Martin during his teen years. How could it be that he and Diane had been married three decades when he only felt like he was thirty-five years old? Most of the time. On the inside at least.

If a day was really like a thousand years to God and a thousand years was like a day, did everything happen at once for God? If time accelerated for Bishop Brewan more and more as he passed the half-century mark of his walk in this world, how fast would it seem to The One who was eternal? It was a question that he considered more and more these days.

Chapter 13

"It's a question I can't answer," Diane was on the cell to Bish as he flew toward Yakutat from Sheldon. "At least not yet."

Bish suppressed a chuckle. His Diane did not give up easily on a project. Her thirty-year marriage to him was evidence of that fact.

"I heard that, Bish."

"Of course you did, Artie. And being all wise you know what made me laugh don't you?"

"Because you heard me say 'Not yet' and you know I won't give up until I have an answer?"

"Like I said, 'all wise.'"

"The journals are so frustratingly vague sometimes and so meticulously detailed at other times. I can't figure out why most of the time." Diane sighed her long-suffering researcher's sigh that wordlessly expressed her inner wish that the rest of the world was as organized and logical as she was.

Bish smiled, but made no sound. How could he have ever deserved such a woman?

"Justice is getting what we deserve," he liked to tell his seminary students. "Mercy is not getting what we deserve. And grace is getting so much more than we could ever hope to deserve." He had Diane because of grace.

He missed her now that he was back on the regular circuit and he could tell that she missed him too. Even though she had called Elder Director Jaegar and encouraged their old friend to get him back in the saddle. He grinned at the thought that she didn't know that he knew.

He wasn't really quite sure how he knew, but he did. Maybe it was Jacob's tone or the timing of his call. Or maybe it was Diane's overacted feigned surprise when he finished the chat with Jaegar and turned to announce, "It's Willie Nelson time."

It didn't matter. He was on the road again, the Marine Highway, and it felt right. All his life he'd had intuitions and presentiments, and ignoring them had led him astray more often than had trusting them. Over the years he had disciplined himself into a pattern of dealing with these occurrences. When he got these hunches he asked himself a few simple questions: "Does the action you believe you are required to take contradict God's will as far as you are able to discern it?" "Are you being called to do something ordinary and easy or something difficult and frightening?" "Has your past prepared you in some way for the future you face now?"

Diane was doing something similar with Aunt Posie's journals, looking for a pattern, a repeated phrase or idea, a contradiction or controversy that would help them understand why his cousin Ran the Man had alienated or been alienated by Uncle Martin and Aunt Posie. She was asking questions but not getting any answers, not yet.

They chatted a little while about the girls and the grandkids, about their hope that there would be visitors to Posie's Perch soon so the family could see the renovations and additions, about Bish's plan to make Yakutat a short stop and then fly to Ketchikan

where he'd ride the ferry to Craig, and Petersburg before returning to Kake. Sometimes he felt like that old bear he might have seen from Ronni and Van's window that night, rambling seemingly aimlessly but with a purpose he alone understood, following a trail he could sense, smell maybe, more than he could see, heading the right way but not certain what to expect along the way, hearing a call and following it even when he was unsure where it led.

Interesting, wasn't it that he had not really seen the bear, not clearly enough to know it really was a bear, but, as he said good-bye to Diane and turned to look out the tiny window of his little ferry cabin, he knew it was a bear. And it was an old bear too.

Chapter 14

Yakutat's airport was a curse and a blessing simultaneously. If Ketchikan was the doorway to the Southeast from the Lower '48, Yakutat was the entry point to the Alaskan mainland. The old airport, built to be part of the United States' defenses during WW II, was increasingly overworked and overwhelmed as the Meltese influx showed no signs of abating. The world had heard the word; Alaska was the final frontier, the land of milk and honey—or at least homes and money—and millions were on their way to making the huge state, more than twice the size of Texas, their new hope, their last hope.

Pastor Suzie Taylor stood among the drivers and greeters, holding a hand-lettered sign that read "Bishop Bishop," the nomenclature she had used from the very first with Brewan. It spoke about both her respect and her affection. Suzie was a Tlingit woman of the old school who believed in tradition. She also believed in progress and innovation. If Yakutat had an avatar, it was Suzie.

"Pastor Taylor," Bishop greeted her with a slight bow, his two palms touching at the fingertips, arms bent at the elbows, a salutation rapidly replacing the handshake in a world with rapidly increasing Eastern influence and international concern about germs from around the planet. Taylor returned the gesture with a slight smile at the corners of her lips and a sparkle in her eyes. How old are you, her face seemed to ask, but her words were kinder.

"Greetings, Bishop. I trust you had a safe sailing?"

"Safe and smooth sailing the whole way, Pastor. God is good all the time."

"All the time, God is good."

The EPIC church in Yakutat was a bright sunny yellow one-story building sitting in the middle of a large gravel parking lot surrounded by a fringe of fireweed and a scattering of brush and trees. The church had been a dingy white the last time Bish visited and his surprise as he walked around the perimeter, taking it all in, chuckling softly to himself, made Taylor smile too.

"What do you think, Bishop?"

"It's brilliant. I think it should be EPIC's official church color. All the Southeast churches should be this color."

He meant it too. Dingy white, barn red, and Sheldon Jackson brown had been the traditional colors for the churches of the Southeast for years, but this yellow was wonderful. It looked like sunshine and laughter and love and hope. Bishop smiled again.

"What is this paint color called?"

"You know paint companies, Bishop. Nothing is simple or clear with them. Orange is always something like "tangerine sunrise" and green is "olive optimism.""

No wonder her congregation loved Suzie. She was sunshine and laughter herself in her own subdued, beneath the surface sort of way. Brewan smiled some more.

"And this yellow is called, what?"

"'Buttery blessing.'"

"No way, Pastor."

"Yes, Bishop. Way."

Never let it be said that God had no sense of humor. They both laughed and tears ran down Bish's face.

Unlike some of his other pastors, Taylor was not a child who expected her bishop to spend at least as much time with her as he did with pastors in villages less easily accessible or in churches troubled by conflicts needing his official presence or deciding voice. She knew he was available if and when he was needed and that was what mattered. If Bish could get her back into school for a couple more degrees, he thought about it, watching her laugh, Suzie Taylor might be a great bishop herself someday for this evolving refrigerator of God's creation.

After a tour of the church and a long lunch in the church's kitchen that the congregation's deacons had insisted on serving, the bishop and the pastor went for a walk down to the waterfront. Neither said anything for the first five minutes, both waiting to let the other begin. Finally, Bishop chose to play the elder card.

"Tell me about it, Pastor Taylor. What mischief has God been up to in your life lately?"

What wonderful mischief it was. Suzie Taylor had met a man. They had been dating for six months now. She thought he might be "the one."

"When do I get to meet the gentleman?"

"Bishop, that's exactly what he is, a gentle man and a gentleman. Bill is the police chief and you can meet him this afternoon if you'd like. We'd both like that."

"The police chief? Are you sure this is a dating relationship and not a job opportunity?" Bish smiled at her and with her.

Taylor had been a nurse and a police officer in previous calls to serve her people. Bish was at least a little concerned that she might be deciding to return to one of those jobs instead of incorporating them into her work for God.

"I'm sure, Bishop. I won't trade the Bible for a badge. I know the difference between the law and the Law."

"Good answer, Suzie."

Police Chief Bill Downing was a good five years younger than Suzie but when she greeted him with a kiss her age dropped by ten. She was a young woman in love, and Bill's eyes proclaimed the love was returned. Bish Brewan was happy for them both and for the church too. Surely, there would be pastor's kids in the future, and churches with children attracted families with children, and lives were shared and fellowship and faith grew up with the families. Back in Pittsburgh and the surrounding area too many congregations were dying as their older members died and were not replaced by the generations of their children and grandchildren.

After lunch and conversation Bish was escorted back to the airport in the chief's police cruiser in time to catch the plane Ketchikan. Bish insisted on sitting up front and wouldn't let them run the siren. That was how rumors got started. "Did you hear the bishop was arrested in Yakutat?" What a call from Jaegar that would inspire.

Chapter 15

Climatologists, seismologists, geologists, and scientists in general were not optimistic about what the next century would bring for the most dominant species on the planet called Earth. The rest of the world agreed. China had reinstated its one-child policy. Mad Max movies weren't fun or funny anymore. Children's shows stopped featuring dinosaurs when the general population realized they might be the next disappearing giants.

Rumors circulated that the government was planning space missions to other planets, seeking new places for humanity to live when Earth was no longer livable. The New Noahs, a group of crackpots determined that God was planning the Great Flood 2, talked about Earth Arks and Space Arks with pseudo-scientific and pretend psychological seriousness that gave people false hope and hindered their willingness to change, to do anything that might even slow the demise of humanity. Alien salvation dreams spurred increased UFO sightings, and hucksters and charlatans made millions by preying upon the fears of millions.

"The more things change," Aunt Posie loved to say, "the more they stay the same." Bish wasn't sure the saying was true in regard to "things," but it certainly rang true in regard to people. People did not want to accept their roles as co-creators of the Kingdom of God. Either they wanted God to do everything for them or they wanted to be supreme rulers themselves. The ambitions of humans had not changed much since Adam and Eve had attempted to trade their roles as beloved children of God and stewards of creation for the crowns of authority and autonomy. Why hadn't the race outgrown its childish insistence that either they were totally in charge of the world or that nothing at all was ever their fault? Why couldn't they grow up and realized they were all in the world together and needed to work together?

Sin. The answer was sin. Sin was an addiction and like all addictions it could not be cured. It could be studied and allayed. It could be calmed and controlled to a point but it could not be eliminated, not until God rebooted the whole system and established a new praxis, not until the New Heaven and the New Earth that John of Patmos had written of in the book of *Revelation* was established.

Bish knew about sin and addiction. "Every worship service on every Sunday in every church should begin like an NA meeting," he told his students back in Pittsburgh. "Hi. My name is Bishop and I'm a sinner. And so are you. We are all sinners. But we are forgiven. Now let's get to work."

That was the way it worked. Or at least the way it was supposed to work. Unfortunately, most of the time people concentrated upon one or more of three other options. They blamed others for their problems and did nothing themselves to remedy them. They blamed themselves to the point of immobility. They claimed that problems and blame were fictions. Evil loved all three responses.

Dr. Brewan looked at his watch. It was time to wrap up the lecture. He took a deep breath and began, "so, you basically have two choices. You can be a servant of the Lord, or you can be a slave to sin. That's it. Two choices. Don't let anyone tell you anything else."

He hesitated a moment, watching the faces on his computer screen. Seventeen first-year seminarians. Wow. How many would make it through? How many would understand? Only God knew.

"Ladies and gentlemen, have a good afternoon. God bless. Keep the faith." He turned off his machine.

Bishop Brewan was not sure why he kept trying to do so many different things. It wasn't just because the church asked him to, not really. It was because he had always had a focus problem. His wife once called him a dilettante, suggesting that maybe he had some form of ADHD, that he couldn't focus or concentrate because there was something inherently wrong with him. He chuckled. Wasn't there something inherently wrong with everyone? Wasn't that what he had just told the class?

Sometimes Diane was right, but he wasn't sure that she was this time. He was interested in so many things, wished that he could do so many things well, and had trouble admitting that there were very few things that he was called to do, that he was equipped to do, much less prepared to do. He chuckled. Wasn't that what he had just told his students? Being prepared, being willing, making the right choices.

A servant of God or a slave to sin. Those really were the only two choices, but the difficulty lay in not making the initial choice, that was not as difficult as some folks suggested. The real challenge was in making the right choice over and over again every day hour after hour, moment after moment, facing one decision after another.

It was indeed a lot like fighting an addiction. You couldn't decide to give up drinking and then never drink again. You couldn't wean yourself from drugs and just stop. You had to stop and stay stopped and work to remain stopped every single day for the rest of your life.

Sin was that way too. You could be so determined to follow the Christ, to serve the living Lord, but your determination had to stretch over a lifetime. You had to not just make the decision, you had to follow the decision, day after day from here to eternity. He chuckled. It sounded like an old movie title, didn't it? He wondered sometimes if that's the way his students heard him. Did he sound like an old movie, like an old vid repeating itself over and over again? His messages, his lectures, did not vary that much. He had one thing to say. Follow the Lord. That was it. Follow the Lord. Today. Tomorrow. For eternity. Do what God calls you to do.

Bish poured himself another cup of blucaf and walked out onto the deck. It was very early. The five hour time difference between Kake and Pittsburgh made live lectures a bit of a challenge sometimes. To teach a class at noon in Pennsylvania, Bish had to begin at 7 o'clock in Kake. It could be a bit of a pain in the posterior. Evening classes, however, made up for it. A class scheduled for 8 o'clock in the evening, Pennsylvania time, began at three in Kake. So it was done by five.

EPIC did not object if Bish decided to pre-tape his lectures when he was traveling, making the circuit throughout the Southeast, but most of the time he really preferred to be able to see the students' reactions, to judge their faces, to understand whether or not they understood. Lectures, he was firmly convinced after all of these years, were the laziest and poorest forms of teaching. The longer a teacher lectured, the more of the students' time he wasted. Students needed to listen, to hear, to understand, to interact, to question, and to speak themselves.

Jesus had understood that different people learn in different ways. That's why he healed different people in different ways. Sometimes he touched people and sometimes he allowed them to touch him. Sometimes he uttered commands. Sometimes he made proclamations and promises. Bish chuckled to himself. How surprised should anyone be that the creator of everything had also created learning styles and teaching styles?

Chapter 16

Diane Mercer Brewan had a heart for the helpless. She stood behind the sliding glass doors now, watching her husband drinking his coffee. He had worried more than she had that moving to Alaska would be difficult for her. He feared that he was asking her to give up her work, her calling from God, but that was certainly not the case.

Here in Alaska there were millions of people who needed help. She knew she was just one worker in an ever-growing vineyard. And that was fine with her. She could not imagine what life would be like without work.

Diane had originally trained to be a librarian, but had later become a special education teacher, an ESL teacher, and an expert researcher. Her God-given gifts of language and laughter endeared her to all of her students, and her skills in listening and counseling insured that their parents loved her too.

She knew that Bish had worried. He was afraid that coming to Alaska might mean she was giving up her work. She smiled and shook her head slightly. No, it only meant she was relocating. People were people and children were children and challenges were challenges. No matter where they lived, they would be plenty for her to do.

She watched her husband moving along the deck railing, not

clutching it as he would have a month earlier, not even touching it really. She was glad that she had called Jaegar. Being back in the field was what Bish needed, whether he knew it or not. Sometimes spouses know their partners better than the partners know themselves, especially after three decades together. Three decades. She thought about that a moment. Over thirty years ago she had met this man and had fallen in love with him, even as he had with her. In fewer than thirty more years they would certainly both be gone, both moved on to the eternal future God had planned for them. Scriptures suggested that marriage did not continue in Heaven, but Diane was sure that friendship did. And that made her heart glad.

Diane walked over to Bish's desk to make sure he had turned the computer off. He had. His cane was leaning against his chair and that made her smile. She knew that the cane would soon be an affectation more than a deed. It would be a mental crutch more than a physical crutch. It would be part of Bish's persona, the word he liked to use, persona, just the way his fedora was part of it, and just the way his rimless glasses were part of it.

Do we create, Diane wondered, an exterior that matches our real interior? Or do we attempt to mold an outward image that makes up for the weaknesses we feel within our souls? Do we try to make the outside match the inside, or do we try to make the outside make up for the inside? Bish would probably say that it was a little bit of both but that was his standard answer to so many of her questions. Things did not have to be mutually exclusive he told her, despite what she knew he told his students so many times. Life was about choices, she knew that. But, she also knew that life was seldom about easy choices.

She was here now with Bish at Posie's Perch. She loved the little cottage looking out on the bay and the long summer had not been unpleasant, but winter was something else. She would much rather spend winter in Arizona with the girls. And with the grandchildren. And with Bish, if she could only get him to move there too, someday.

Bish often joked about retirement, "I was tired yesterday," he would say. "And I am re-tired today, but I am not ready to be retired tomorrow."

Diane did not think she was tired yet, but she was growing weary. World-weary was what Aunt Posie called it in the journals and Diane liked that phrase, world-weary. As Posie used it, it meant tired of trying to compensate for or correct the stupid silly mistakes other people made every day.

Bish had once said to her that he expected people to be assholes in life. He understood that. It was not assholes, he claimed, that irritated him. It was folks who were assholes and proud of it that got his dander up.

That's not quite the way that Diane thought. "Clueless," was the word she used. So many folks were so clueless and did not seem to be seeking clues. Perhaps "oblivious" would be a good word for it too. They wandered through their lives with no purposes beyond procreation and recreation. They ate and they slept. They worked and they played. They had no feeling for the past, and they had no goals for the future, except for earning enough money to be able to work less and play more.

She could not understand how they failed to understand the need for community and family and society and fellowship that were essential parts of the human soul. They all disagreed with the poet John Donne who had declared that no person was an island separate from the world, that we were all pieces of a continent called humanity. They really thought they were individual and unique entities, laws unto themselves, beings endowed with the right to change the world for their own pleasure and profit.

Diane and Bish had talked about it often. It was Satan's oldest divide and conquer strategy. Most of the time people experienced the love of God through experiencing the love of others. The more evil could separate one from the love of others the more those folks could be alienated from God's love. Isolation, abuse, bad weather, excessive video and computer usage, anything that shrank a person's world could be used to shrink their perception of God's amazing love too.

Diane had lived too long to believe there were limitations upon God's amazing grace. She had seen too many things, too many miracles, in too many places and situations to ever say something was impossible for God. God's love was so impossibly big that the impossible became infinitely possible in his mercy and grace.

Diane and Bish had met when they were both still students in Pittsburgh. They married when she was 20 and he was 21. Five years later their first daughter was born, and three years after that their second. They had lived together and loved together and laughed together and learned together more than half of their lives, and they had too many more years ahead, she hoped and prayed, for either of them to be world-weary now. Maybe in another ten or twenty years that would be acceptable, but not now, not when they were facing what very well could be the biggest challenge of their lives.

The girls liked to tease Diane that her love for the helpless, that her affinity for the underdog, had been the main motivating factor in her union with their father. Both knew that sometimes Bish was just a big kid, a man on the outside but still a child on the inside, a fellow with all the fears and insecurities and stresses known to children. She laughed about it with them, knowing that on the inside she was sometimes just a little girl.

As the girls aged, they too would understand that the human exterior ages much more rapidly than the human spirit. They would grow to comprehend that part of us, our spirit or soul or our psyche, yearns eternally for a mother's warm embrace, for a father's hug, for a sister or brother's smile. "Children of God" was the phrase she had heard her husband use often and "children" was what we always are, she told herself. Children. Of. God.

Diane slid open the glass door now. "Hey, Hoppy. How's it going?"

"Better," her husband smiled at her. "Better, now that you're here."

They drank their coffee on the deck and chatted for nearly half an hour before the rain started again and Bish joked it was a new record in Kake, thirty minutes without rain. He guessed God still did work miracles.

Chapter 17

"That dog is not a dog," he heard the whispered words again. He heard them every time they walked down to the docks. He heard them every time he walked any place with his large canine companion, and they always made him smile. "That is not a dog. That is a wolf."

"Did you see that animal? That is not a dog. That's a wolf."

"Oh my, look at that. That's one big what? Dog?""

His dog was not a dog and he knew it and that was just fine with him. Because his dog was not a dog, the owner of the restaurant where he washed dishes let him sleep there at nights. The not dog would prevent break-ins or at least continued break-ins if anyone was foolish enough to attempt the first time.

Because his dog was not a dog, no one bothered him if he fell asleep at the docks sitting on one of the benches in the rain. Policeman would look at that not dog from a distance and see its collar with its little brass license and then pretend it was a dog because that was safer, safer for everyone.

Because his dog was not a dog no one followed him from the bars at night to rob him. Because his dog was not a dog no one yelled or honked warnings when he walked down the middle of the street, too drunk to stay on the sidewalk. Because his dog was not a dog, his life seemed better, bolder, bigger than it ever had before. Because his dog was not a dog, he felt like a man.

"Wolf," they said. "Wolf, not a dog." But he knew better. It was not a dog, they were right about that, but it was not a wolf either.

The third day he was in the caves, the day he was feeling trapped, buried alive, ready to scream and run, even though he fought to keep any of it from showing on the outside, the dog that was not a dog had come to him in the early darkness. They had all seen it standing beyond the cave's mouth, beyond the flickering fire, and then he had whispered, "Wolf, though no wolf."

They had all been afraid, all except him. He had not been afraid, no, not afraid. He had been enthralled, fascinated, captivated by the fire in the creature's eyes that was more than just the reflections of the cave fire, that was more than just fire on the outside, that was fire from the inside too. So he had walked past the fire, out of the cave and stood before it silently, staring, waiting for something, something he didn't know what, but waiting for something, something to happen.

And something did happen. The dog that was not a dog spoke to him, spoke to him softly, spoke to him softly but clearly.

"We are together now," it said. "Come with me."

And he knew it was not a dog because dogs don't talk. And he knew it was not a wolf because wolves do not talk either. So he followed. Gathering up his small batch of belongings, he left the cave with his new friend.

In his head he named his new companion Nada Dogg because he thought that was funny. It made him chuckle and Nada looked at him when he chuckled and Nada seemed to smile too.

Every day that a ferry came in they went together down to watch the boat unload. Some days they went to watch even when there was no boat. He wasn't sure why, wasn't sure why they went on those days, but his friend would stir and raise up on his paws and move from the corner where he slept, ignoring the cooks and dishwashers, and walk to stand by the kitchen door until the man took off his apron and his hairnet and said to the others, "I'll be back soon."

The dog that was not a dog had not spoken again. He never barked and he never growled. He never snarled, nor whined, nor whimpered. He never wagged his tail. At night he curled up at the man's feet and he usually fell asleep before the man did, but many times when the man awoke in the middle of the night he would see Nada staring at him, with faint fire flickering in his eyes. He knew that should trouble him but it did not and he felt safe sleeping there.

Sitting beside the dog that was not a dog, he would speculate about what they were waiting for, watching for. He had many theories. It might be the girl, Trixie. It might be that nosy Bishop. It might be state troopers. Or it might be The Teacher.

A few times he tried to guess. He asked questions. "Is it Trixie? Is it that bastard Bishop? Is it cops? Is it the teacher?"

The animal never answered. He never growled nor smiled. He just sat and then he would stand up and turn away and they would return to dishwashing and sleeping. And this went on for weeks.

The dishwashing job did not pay much but the restaurant owner allowed them both to eat in the kitchen. At night he washed his clothes in one of the big stainless steel sinks and he bathed in another. The owner didn't know or didn't care. The other employees stayed away from the two friends and that was fine too.

He thought about opening a bank account but decided not to. He kept his money in his shoes now and in a little bag he wore between his jeans and his boxers. At night he slept with it inside his shirt. In the mornings before anyone else came to the restaurant he would remove a few bills and place them in his pockets for daily expenses. When he was paid, in cash, he put the money in those pockets until he was alone to add it to his stash.

Sometimes he would ask Nada Dogg, "Do we have enough?"

But Nada never answered.

The ferry was late today and he thought about leaving. Would one day really matter? But his friend was sleeping so soundly that he decided to stay, at least for a little while longer. It would be wrong to spoil his record now. He had been patient and persistent for how long? Forty days? Was it really forty days? Maybe, yes, probably, forty days.

He could see the *Taku II* now on the horizon. It was going to be nearly an hour late, not usual but not unusual either, not with the way the water was any more.

He thought about buying a burger from the food stand along the dock. They could split it while they waited, but the animal did not stir and so he sat still.

Feeling the creature's fur brushing his arm, he awoke. The ferry was nearly docked. With his companion he moved into the shadows behind the terminal, between the parked trucks where he waited each day. Where he could see without being seen.

It took fifteen minutes to dock and tie up the *Taku II* before it began to unload, and then for passengers for to disembark another fifteen minutes or so, but the two watchers did not give up. They waited.

Then the reloading began as cars and trucks drove onto the ferry and passengers pulled their suitcases down the metal grate ramp, and the siren warnings sounded, alerting visitors that it was time to leave, notifying travelers it was time to be boarded, telling the watchers they had waited for nothing.

But then Nada growled and the man followed his gaze upward, watching as a large raven lifted off the top of the boat and glided toward the dock..

He felt it in his bones, in the hair standing out on the back of his neck and he waited another minute. The last horn sounded and the purser was gathering up his paperwork to walk up the ramp to the ferry when a lone figure came sauntering down, carrying only a faded backpack. He wore his gray hair tied into braids and his mustache and beard were even whiter than before but The Teacher was easily recognizable.

"It's him," the dog that was not a dog spoke softly.

"Yes," Muck nodded. "It is him."

As quietly as an angry man and a dog that is not a dog can follow, they fell in behind the new arrival, staying in the shadows and the growing fog, staying just far enough behind to hide from human eyes.

Chapter 18

"According to Aunt Posie's Journal," Diane greeted Bish as he came through the door, "your cousin Randolph would not be the first in your family to be involved in shamanism."

"I am not sure I want to hear this," Bish stared at his wife.

"I'm sure you probably do not want to hear this," Diane smiled a sad smile, "but you need to hear it."

They sat inside, in front of the double glass doors that opened onto the deck, listening to the rain fall, trying to imagine Aunt Posie writing the words, sitting in this same room before it had the deck and the doors, listening herself to the rain on the roof as she wrote the words that she hoped no one would ever need to read. They were not happy words:

Today it happened again. Big Bear told Daisy the raven had spoken to him down by the water where he and Martin were fishing. He said Martin heard it too, but when I asked him, my husband just laughed and said Brewan has an active imagination. This is the third time her husband has shared such an event with Daisy and she is frightened. She wants to tell Pastor but her husband says no. He knows the old tales and fears they will be driven from the village. Or worse.

I am not sure what to think about Martin. I never knew him to lie to me before. Is he frightened? Did Big Bear make it all up? Is one of them crazy? Or both? My spirit is uneasy tonight and I fear I will not sleep. Perhaps Violet was right. Maybe leaving here was for the best.

"That's it?" Bish stared at his wife. "No more?"

"Not that I've found yet, but isn't this enough? Or too much?"

"What do you mean?" He knew what she meant but couldn't say it himself.

"Your family," she watched him carefully, "is nuts. How could they do this?"

Bish shook his head. "I don't know. I guess 'nuts' is right."

"Bish, your own father. And Posie's husband. The man who lived in this house." Diane shuddered. "Who were those people? Really?"

Brewan watched her eyes now as he spoke with a calmness he did not feel inside. "They were and are just people like anyone else. Just because they were tempted or tested doesn't mean a thing. We are all tempted and tried many times in life."

"Not like that." Diane shook her head and turned away.

"Artie, honey, you know what I told you about the bird on the boat."

"That was a dream. You were partly asleep. You said so yourself."

"And the little girl who heard the Trickster hassling me? Was she asleep too?"

Diane turned to glare at him. "Maybe she was. Or maybe you dreamed her up too."

Bish took a slow deep breath. She was scared, frightened by a story in a book written ages ago. "It's just a story, Diane. You know how Posie can be. She probably misunderstood or mis-remembered it as she wrote it down." He watched her face, her face that was torn between wanting to believe something she knew wasn't true and not wanting to believe something she feared was too true.

"But what if it is a family thing?"

"What if it is, Artie? You know me, and I know you, and we both know our girls. We all made our choices a long time ago. We aren't switching teams now. Or ever."

"But, Hoppy, what about your dad? And Uncle Martin?" Diane had tears in her eyes now, so Bish had to hide his.

"Both good men, Diane. Both good Christian men. Trust me. I've known them my whole life."

"I want to burn these journals. I don't want them in the house anymore."

"Whatever you decide, Artie. You do what you think is best."

"I hate you, Bishop Brewan. You know I can't destroy them. They're history, family history, and I have to get to the bottom of this."

"I hate you too, Artie, whole bunches. I can't imagine living without you to hate. Hating you is the best part of my life."

It worked. They were both laughing and then hugging and then wiping the tears from their eyes. Diane coughed and blew her nose into one of the tissues she always had in her pocket and Bish wiped his eyes with his sleeve. He poured them each fresh cups of blucaf and they sat side by side, each holding a mug of blucaf in one hand and their best friend's hand in the other.

After a few moments, Bish spoke again, "Seriously, destroy them if you believe that's for the best."

"Oh, I will. Trust me. If I decide that's best .But I have to learn more first."

"I understand and I do trust you, but you have to be careful, Artie."

"No pasa nada. I will be very careful."

There wasn't much more to say. Not yet. Diane would keep reading, keep searching, and they both would pray a lot. They'd trust each other and they'd trust God more.

The rest of the evening they avoided the topic, both understanding that speculation would be idle at best and nerve-wracking and both aware that sometimes the opposite of doing good and being good is being fearful and being afraid to do what needs to be done. If Aunt Posie believed it was important enough to preserve and if she left that written account where they could discover it so easily, then a time would come when they needed to know what they had just learned. It might not be a good time, but it would be a time God would ultimately use for the good. God was like that, they both knew.

Chapter 19

She'd watched him for weeks, certain but not entirely certain, sure but not sure enough, but now she was positive. Even the way he walked wasn't quite right for Briggs. It was close but not close enough, not for her, not for one who had lived it already herself.

He was trying, obviously, most of the time. Maybe it wasn't his failure, really, but The Boss'. The Boss tried to treat him like Briggs, but he couldn't. Not quite. He smiled too much. Chuckled too much and growled too little. Most of it was body language she decided.

She hailed him softly but firmly as he passed her desk. "Hey. 'Briggsy.'"

He had not been watching her because he already knew. This wasn't his first rodeo, not by a long shot, and he knew what to look for. In the eyes, at the corners of the mouth, the set of the shoulders, the tilt of the chin. And of course there was the aura if you knew how to see through the shield.

"Hey yourself," his words were as quiet as hers. "It took you long enough."

She studied him. "I know you don't I?"

"So you don't know after all? Not all of it at least. That's sort of funny. You'll think so too when you figure it out. Secretary. What a sense of humor he has." He walked away chuckling.

So he knew her better than she knew him. He knew why The Boss had made her his secretary, knew how humiliating it was for her, and how funny The Boss thought that was. How high was he? Who was he? One of the fixed or maybe even one of the firm?

How worried was Boss if he was bringing in the firm now? How close to the time could it be? She stirred in her seat uncomfortably. Stupid padded ass and stupid tight clothes. Was he even going to tell her? Or was this a test too? She was so sick of tests that she could puke. If she could figure out just how that worked. Some things that should be so natural and so easy weren't either.

Maybe the first time was more of a challenge? Like diving or flying or traveling through the wall? There was so much to remember and monitor until it became automatic. The breathing. The pulse. The blinking and the winking. The pretended pain when you got cut or hit your head or stubbed your toe. The emotions, so many emotions, to match the emotions of the others around you. It took so long to master it.

Of course there was the walking and the talking too, walking that felt like you were wearing a cement suit and talking like shouting through sand. None of it was easy or automatic or natural. She wished she had her old self back, and she leaked a tear without having to force it. Her old self was probably long gone by now, fuel for the furnace or food for the firm. It was better to not wish for the impossible. Be the secretary, she whispered to herself. Be the secretary so he doesn't decide to make you something worse.

Chapter 20

Trying to become a new person is not easy, Beatrice Foster told herself. Nothing worth doing is easy, Ronni had told her repeatedly, but sometimes…sometimes she wondered if any of it was worth it. Had the old Trixie been all that bad? Really?

Hadn't she just been a little young, a little stupid, and a little too trusting? And wasn't that what you were supposed to be when you were young, before you learned? And was it her fault that she had run into bad teachers, poor role models, strong influences that seemed fun and cool and okay? How could she have known how rotten and using folks could be? She wasn't even halfway through her twenties yet.

She stopped a moment to do the math. She'd lied so many times about her age that sometimes she forgot not only how old she was telling folks she was, but how old she really was too. Nope. Not halfway through her twenties yet. But almost now.

The bell above the door of Veronica's Attic rang now as Bea's favorite customer came in smiling. He wasn't really a customer, she reminded herself, because he never bought anything, and he wasn't her favorite because "We don't have favorites. All of our customers are valued and valuable," Ronni reminded her at least twice a day.

Still, she was delighted to see him and he returned her smile with fervor. "I brought tuna sandwiches, rice salad, and blupop. Sound okay?"

"Sounds great." She thought he actually cared. He bought the food and he brought the food and he must have chosen what he likes, but he still wants me to be happy. Maybe Ronni is right. There might be hints of Heaven on Earth. Or maybe he just wants some candy and thinks I'm too stupid to see it.

Why do I have to do that? She almost smacked herself. Why can't I just enjoy the moment? Van would say I am damaged, that we are all damaged and in constant need of repair, and he might be right. Not that he's gonna hear that from me. He's a dick anyway.

She brightened her face and came from behind the counter to give her favorite customer a hug and a quick kiss on the cheek. He blushed, he always did, and she loved that. He would be shocked if he heard her calling Van a dick.

He wouldn't hear it. Trixie might say dick or prick or jerk or asshole, but Bea never would. She was not that kind of girl. Remember that, she told herself, Bea is not that kind of girl.

What would Teacher say and snide boy Aaron and the stupid bishop if they knew she was dating a poet? Or almost dating. He had never asked her out or taken her anyplace alone, without Ronni and Van. Still, she wished they did know so they could see she was not who they thought she was. She had value and was valuable too. Ronni had told her that there was a difference between a slow learner and a non-learner, "a fine line," she called it. Maybe she had tripped over and slipped over the line in the past, but she was walking carefully now.

The shop didn't close for lunch but she was a salaried employee now and allowed to eat while working and she still got paid for the time. That seemed cool enough she thought. It didn't make up entirely for having to work every Saturday, but Ronni told her that was part of being "assistant manager," and the extra Ameca and a half an hour was cool too. She wasn't going to hang around here forever, but she had started saving a little and could see herself taking off in six months or a year.

Bea sort of surprised herself with that thought. When had she ever planned six months or a year in advance before? It had always been either "right now" or "someday" for her. What had Van called it? "Immediate gratification" and "pie in the sky by and by." He was a dick but maybe not a stupid dick. And maybe she still was being unfair because he had rejected her candy when she first moved in with them. In retrospect that had been stupid. Retrospect? Where had she learned that word she wondered.

"Have you heard anything I've said?" Her favorite customer was watching her quizzically, trying not to laugh but obviously amused by something.

"Of course I have," she almost flared, but she calmed herself. "No, my mind was wandering. Sorry."

"We all do it," he laughed. "Glad you're back now."

The first time he'd come into the shop he was looking for bowties, and she thought he must be some sort of computer geek working for Kagi or maybe a junior banker or something. Who wore bowties anymore? Maybe somebody from the Civil War or one of Columbus' ships or somebody from France?

She'd laughed, thinking he was joking, and said, "Sorry, no bowties, no suits of armor, and no Roman togas. We sold out of all that stuff last week."

"Do you know anybody in town who might have them?" He was serious?

"Can't imagine it. Not a big demand for that stuff in Sheldon, Alaska."

A week later he'd returned wearing a bow tie and a big smile. "Found it online. A guy in Anchorage who had a collection passed away and I bought them all."

"So that's a bow tie?" She had never seen one, at least not in person.

"It's not a suit of armor nor a toga," he grinned.

Nor? He said "nor"? She tried to smile, a little worried he might be dangerous, a little mental maybe. "I see that. It's not."

"Just wanted you to see it in case any ever came in. You might save them for me?"

"I guess I could, if the boss lets me."

"I thought you were the boss. I should have known." He blushed, trying to be smooth. "Bosses are never as pretty as you."

He kept coming back and he kept saying things like that. Ronni heard him and told Van and he made an excuse to come in and listen the next time the fellow returned.

"Oh, my goodness," he laughed after the favorite noncustomer left, "he sounds like a love sick time traveler. I think it used to be called 'Smitten.'"

Now he and Ronni teased her every day about her "suitor." She'd blushed herself when she looked up that word. "Suitor" sort of suited him, she decided.

"Sweets for the sweet," he grinned as they finished lunch and he pulled two dark chocolate bars from the lunch bag. She'd never imagined she'd meet, let alone have feelings for a poet, she told herself, but he was starting to grow on her. Who was this Robert Service guy he was talking about now? She'd have to look that up too. And why had the university hired a poet anyway? That still didn't seem like a smart thing. Not when the world was all falling apart.

"Thanks," she said and smiled. She loved dark chocolate.

Chapter 21

If this continued much longer, he might drown himself. He had done it before and he could do it again. Along with many others he had rushed down a cliff and died in the sea when Jesus cast them out of a possessed man. Drowning had been quick at least. This might last forever.

What was the boy waiting for? He whined at the kid, afraid talking again would just distract him, would make him think about the creature he called Nada Dogg and forget about the one he called Teacher. The boy just rubbed the fur between the wolf's ears and whispered, "Not yet. Not here. Not now."

Then when? He had helped the idiot follow the Teacher for almost a week. There had been several opportunities. No witnesses. No place for the older man to run. No reasons to say, "No."

But the spineless young man kept saying, "No."

Killing a person was easy. The kid had a knife. He had his teeth. The two of them would need just a few seconds and it would be over. The Teacher and his clumsy, ineffectual ways would be over, and a new Teacher, Muck the Teacher, would be born. Born of blood and death and guilt and anger and fear, he would be easier to control and steer than the Teacher was now.

That was the wolf's assignment, and he would remain a wolf until it was complete because he knew better than to try to escape. Escape never worked. How long had he been a fish after leaving that stupid pig until a fisherman finally caught him? It had seemed like a million years, swimming around, avoiding bait and nets, and bigger fish. It had almost made him wish he were a pig again. Almost.

If this went well though, if The Boss was happy with his performance, his success, then he might finally get a real chance to have a human body again and an opportunity for promotion. A wolf had a right to dream, no?

"Nada, come on. He's headed back to his room again. Tonight might be the night."

Yeah. Sure. How many times had he heard that? If only death were the issue he would do it himself. He could run and jump and snap and tear and it would be done. Teacher would be dead. But death was not the primary goal. It was birth, the birth of one more dangerous and more determined and more deadly than Teacher. The lad had to kill once before he could kill again and again, before he made his Teacher look like an amateur by the number of victims he left behind, by the number of lives he ruined.

The wolf sighed, startling Muck with the sound. He rose onto his four feet and followed the boy following the man. It was going to be another long night. Maybe there would be a hamburger later or at least a bowl of beer. The kid had no concept of what wolves really ate. At least that was good.

Chapter 21

Jackie Jaxon came from a long line of carvers. Her great, great uncle had been one of the best carvers in the Southeast in the last century. Her father, gone with so many others in the Edgecombe Disaster, had given in when she was fourteen and begun her training in the traditional carving ways of her family, clan, and tribe. She was determined, he saw, and she would learn from others if she did not learn from him.

He had never known a carver who was a woman, and he had never heard of one either, but he was proud that his daughter was so determined, and from the start so talented. She learned quickly. By the time he was killed, Jackie was still a few weeks short of her twentieth birthday, but she was better than he had ever been.

Jackie thought of her father now, as she talked with Bishop Brewan who had come to visit, bringing an unusual request. She had never carved a cane before, but there was no reason she could not design it the way he was requesting. The big problem might be how much she could charge him for the work. She was very busy with the boat for the Alaskan Native Brotherhood center in Sheldon and hated to be distracted from it, but this was a paying job.

"How soon do you need it and how much do you want to spend?"

Bishop Brewan smiled and chuckled. "Jackie. We went to school together. Your mother and my mother danced together at the potlatches when we were children. We almost went to the prom together our junior year in high school. I know you are busy and I trust your honesty and integrity."

Muck it. She wasn't going to make much on this. Oh well. Hoppy traveled a lot. Maybe others would see her work that way and she'd get a few orders.

"A month. At least. And two hundred Amecas."

"Two hundred?"

"Because you are a friend. Two hundred."

"Done. Now or upon completion?"

"Half now. Half upon completion."

"Done. Thank-you, Jackie."

"Just don't hurt yourself, Hoppy."

"Of course not, Jackie."

Later she would think she should have said, "Nor anybody else," but that might have been a deal breaker. The Bishop Brewan she'd known her whole life still tried to be an honest man.

She thought about their pasts as she watched him walk down the short lane from her shop next to the home that had been her parents and her grandparents but would never belong to children of hers. He didn't seem to be limping. Why did he really need a cane at all? Probably, he did not. He just wanted one. That was Hoppy, too.

In some parts of the world it might have seemed strange that her father and Hoppy's parents had all died in a common tragedy so close to home after traveling to so many different and dangerous places separately for work and family and vacations. They had not been friends, just acquaintances connected only through their children, and had been in Sitka that day for different reasons. As far as Jackie and Hoppy could ever discover, neither family had even known the other was in town. The Jaxons had been meeting a potential totem pole client and the Brewans had been negotiating a deal with the new fish canning plant.

Only Jackie's mother had survived, of the four parents, and Jackie knew that had never felt like a blessing. "Survivor's guilt," Hoppy taught her it was called, had made her final decade in the world a hellish journey peppered with pills and awash in alcohol. Her death had been a relief to her daughter and in being so had passed the guilt on to the next generation.

Jackie had never married, but she was not lonely. She had her work and her friends and her work. That was enough. She smiled, "If you'd been twins, Hoppy Brewan, things might have been different." But that was just wishful thinking. Anybody could have a husband, she reminded herself, but having a lifelong friend was rare.

Chapter 22

Few people with no experience outside a rain forest understood how highly developed were its systems of water collection, distribution and drainage. When it rained in the Tongass Rain Forest, the water fell and flowed and the forest flourished, but when the rain stopped there was an immediate beginning of drought. For millennia the rain had fallen and the forest had prospered, but in The Melt everything was different.

Most of the time rain fell even more frequently and in greater volume than it had in previous centuries, but sometimes the rains stopped for greater periods too, and when that happened the fear of forest fires was widespread. Natives of the land understood that the ground drained quickly and the grass browned and dried, and they were careful after a week without rain and even more careful after a month. They didn't burn garbage in their backyard trash barrels when dry times came, and they didn't toss aside cigarette butts as they hiked along paths in the drying woods. Unfortunately, many of the Melties did not understand this.

Refugees from so many different lands and climes, the Melties had come to Alaska to start new lives in a place as alien to them as a different planet. There were bears that lived in the forest and ate berries and salmon and people. There were fish that lived in fresh water and then swam into the sea and returned to the fresh streams to die. There were birds that could and would carry off your unguarded sandwich or pet cat.

Brightly painted wooden poles bore frightening faces and strange animals and told tales they could not read. Men went out in expensive boats with the most sophisticated technology and advanced fishing equipment ever invented, and disappeared without a trace. Women educated their children and ran businesses and danced in Russian costumes from their ancestors' eras. People prospered and people starved. People loved and people hated for past joys and wrongs passed on in songs. People gathered to pray and to play, to eat and to implore, to debate and to dance, to remember and to remonstrate, often in the same town hall meetings.

Sometimes it was too much if you were a little Meltese girl. Sometimes you desperately grabbed anything from your past and refused to let go, even if the past was not that long ago.

"I want to go to church to see Mr. Bear."

"Why, child? There is church every week. Why now?" Her mother worked twelve hour shifts in the Kagi blueberry plant and her husband worked the same hours in the fields. They were lucky to have a few precious hours on Sundays when they could all be together, when they might cook and eat and play and sleep. When they could pretend their lives were not exhausting, when they could ignore their aching joints and empty purses and pretend life was not nearly as scary as they knew it was.

"Mr. Bear talks to birds. I like him. And he scares bad men away too."

Her mother smiled. "Yes, he does. I will talk with your father. Perhaps we can go to church soon, but not today. It is too late today."

"But soon then?" She was persistent like her grandmother had been, her mother remembered, and like her late uncle and her aunts. She was a good girl.

"Yes, soon. I will talk to your father. But soon. You go outside now. Watch the food on the fire."

When the fire leapt the circle of rocks, aided by a breeze that seemed to magically appear from a cloudless sky, the little girl watched it move like a snake along the edges of the path that led down to the shoreline shack where the salmon was smoked. It seemed alive and alert and she followed it, dancing back and forth on one foot and then the other, trying to catch it, not realizing it did not stay snuffed out but, instead, came back to life behind her. She did not fear it nor worry until it climbed the walls of the smokehouse and she knew it was going to steal their food.

"Mommy, Dad," she screamed as she turned back toward their little house nestled among dozens of identical little homes built from recycled pallets from the barges. "Mommy, Dad."

They were out of the house in an instant and they instantly saw what she did not see. The salmon was in danger but so was she. The fired had encircled her now and was growing quickly higher and thicker. Her father wrapped a bandana around his face as he rushed toward her and her mother threw the bucket of dishwater by the door on him as he ran but they both knew it was too late. He could not outrace the flames.

Feeding on the grass and brindle brush the fire roared toward the shore, driven by the increasing wind away from the houses but toward their only child, their only reason for enduring this awful new world and life they faced every day. They heard her scream once, "No. Stop it," and that was all. The fire was gone and the smokehouse was gone and their daughter was gone.

Moaning, on her knees, the mother rocked back and forth. Sobbing, the father turned left and right, seeking, searching, but finding nothing. He circled the ashes of the smokehouse, dreading what he might find, but he found nothing. Their agony was intense and immediate and awful, and their cries brought the neighbors running.

Different voices would tell the story differently, to the news vid team, to their friends, to their own children and grandchildren, different versions from different perspectives and worldviews and different memories, but all would agree on one thing. The agony of the parents was blessedly short-lived.

"No. Stop it," they heard the cry again. "Put me down, you bird. Put me down."

And the largest eagle they had ever seen or would ever see came sailing over their house to alight and deliver their only child, unscathed by the fire but very upset and very frightened. The bird set the child down as if she were made of the most fragile most valuable material on Earth and rose immediately to fly from sight faster than any eagle they had ever seen or would see.

One old Meltese man, a neighbor who had never spoken to them, or to any of the neighbors before, spoke now the thought they were all sharing, "God not done with that little girl yet. Got plans for her."

And nobody argued.

Chapter 23

Jacob Jaegar was worried about his credibility. No one had complained, and he had not done anything wrong. Perhaps, though, his conscience told him, he had not done all the right that he could have, should have, done for the whole mess up in Southeast Alaska. It had been troubling him for several days now, keeping him awake at night sometimes, and he decided he could not put off taking action any longer.

He had never been to Southeast Alaska. How, therefore, could he pretend to be an expert on the area? How could he be a good resource for Bishop Brewan? How could he sit in on important meetings where life-changing decisions were made, decisions that affected thousands of people, if he had never been to the region where they lived? It just wasn't right.

Jacob knew that he was not really a traveler. He had done fieldwork in his time, of course, but it had never suited him the way this desk job suited him. In his imagination he wanted to be a field man. But every time he went to the field he realized he really wanted to be a desk man. Papers and statistics and logistics, those were his things. Those were where his God-given gifts came into play, and he should be happy with that. Yet, somehow, there was something else his soul said he needed to do.

When he tried to analyze it, it all seemed to go back to that telephone call from Diane Brewan. Diane had trusted him. She had counted on him to do what was best for Bishop and for herself, and he certainly had endeavored to do exactly that. He had listened, and he had counseled, and he had taken counsel. He agreed to let Bish go back into the field on a limited basis at first and then gradually increased his friend's time and efforts until he was back into the full flying of a regular schedule. He had done his job.

He had done his job, but that was all that he had really done. He had not followed through with as much humanity, with as much love, or with as much concern as he wished he had. He wanted to be a better boss, a better supervisor, and a better friend. Sometimes he told himself that he was none of these things because he was too busy or because he didn't know how. At other times he feared that the truth was that he just did not care enough. Oh, he cared on the inside but he didn't care on the outside. He wanted to do his job and be left alone and he wanted to leave others alone to do their jobs too, as long as they did then exactly the way he thought they should be done, he chuckled to himself now. He was just a little bit of a control freak, but he had learned over the many years that he had sat behind that desk that if he didn't exert some control that there were some folks who simply would wander astray, forgetting their charges, forgetting their calls, and becoming lost in the mishmash mess that was the world of The Melt.

So, Jacob Jaegar was going to go to Alaska. When? Soon. And when was soon? Soon was soon. That was all he could say. He had made the decision now and he was going to pray about the timing. He had no qualms about the necessity of the trip. Yet, he wasn't sure about the timing, not quite sure at least, not yet. Perhaps he was just stalling, trying to put off enacting the decision by pretending that making the decision was all that counted, but he knew better than that, didn't he? Of course he did. The first step of solving any problem was admitting that one had a problem, but that was only the first step. There were plenty of other steps to follow. If he wanted to follow in the footsteps of his Lord and Savior, Jesus Christ, he had so many more steps to take and so many more patterns to follow. He knew that.

Maybe if he at least picked the dates that would help. What

month was going to be best? A quick perusal of his calendar revealed that best was indeed the proper term. There was no good. There was no better. There was only the best, the best in terms of the least bad, the least inconvenient, the least impossible within a schedule that was impossible every day.

Pittsburgh had survived much more successfully than many other small cities in the time of The Melt. It would never again be the steel city that it had been ages ago. It would never be a major airline hub or a big player in any of the industries that The Melt had helped prosper. There were no diamond mines in Pittsburgh. You couldn't grow many blueberries in Pittsburgh. Most of the farmland in the area was already being farmed. There was not a lot of room for growth.

Jaegar understood, however that sometimes change itself was growth. The old concept of working smarter instead of working harder had kept Pittsburgh going in the last hundred years, at least. Carnegie Mellon had gained worldwide reputation as an educational center for aspiring actors and entertainers. The University of Pittsburgh, Pitt, trained attorneys and mathematicians sought after by the most progressive companies on the planet. The city's long standing tradition of philanthropy had not suffered because of The Melt, but rather it had increased. Pittsburgh Pennsylvania people were generous people. They believed in sharing their blessings.

Wasn't that, after all, why we were put on this planet? Jacob Jaegar asked himself this on an almost daily basis. Why was I put on this planet? Why here? Why now? These were the questions that gave him direction and guidance and hope. He hoped every day to better fulfill the purposes for which God had created him. He worked every day to be a better Jacob Jaegar, to be the best Jacob Jaegar that he could be.

Now he had to make a change. He had to go into the field. He was not sure exactly why, and he was not sure exactly when, but he was sure. He was certain. He had to go. To Alaska.

Part of the problem, he knew, was the expense. He had a travel budget. The board would understand. In fact, there were probably members who wondered why he did not go to Alaska at least once a year. They would have in his position. They would go to "check up" on Bishop Brewan. They would be getting "the lay of the land." It would help them do their jobs better, they would say. And they would be right. Still, it cost money, money that Jacob Jaegar thought might be used in better ways, even though right now he could not specify exactly what those better ways were.

Maybe money was just an excuse? Maybe he was not being as faithful as he should be? God kept the EPIC church going in The Melt. Budgets were tight, of course, but they were not running out of money. People of faith were givers. In times of trouble they were good givers, even better than they were in normal times. The problem now was that the normal times were troubled times and it looked like that might be the case for the foreseeable future. The Melt was not going away.

Jaegar looked at the pile of reports and articles on the right corner of his desk. The news was not good. Statistics were alarming. Things were bad and they were getting steadily, rapidly, worse. The National Weather Service surveys and analyses suggested that the planet's weather was going to be totally unpredictable for at least the next half decade. After that, well, after that predictions varied. Some said there would indeed be a new Ice Age. Others believed that global warming would be pandemic. The biggest group of scientists suggested that unpredictability was the only thing really predictable. Pittsburgh might have Pittsburgh weather today and Miami weather tomorrow and Anchorage weather the day after that. And the situations in Miami and Anchorage were very likely to be just as mercurial..

In Alaska so far the changes had contributed to an increased growing season, but in many places this was not the case. Wheat crops and corn crops had shown slight but steady declines over the last twenty-five years. Fruit growers, on the other hand, had suffered catastrophe after catastrophe. Sudden frosts and even snow in Florida in July destroyed orange production three years in the last ten. Everything connected with grapes and grape growing had become chaotic. Wine? Maybe this year and maybe not. Raisins? Not now, not after this freeze. Several of Jagger's favorite Northeast and Lake

Erie wineries had gone out of business in just the last two years. The entire Great Lakes wine region had lost nearly one third of its business in the same amount of time.

And there was the problem of the bees. In the first half of the 21st century, scientists had been sounding the alarm that there was something wrong with the bees. They were dying at alarming rates. Folks with the allergies did not mourn the loss, but those who understood pollination and the important part bees play in agriculture became, justifiably, quite worried. The years since then had proved that their concerns were valid.

Then too, Jaegar sighed, there was the problem of the permafrost. What was going to happen as more and more of the carbon hoarding land thawed out? General consensus seemed to be that the effects of The Melt would be multiplied. Those expecting an Ice Age predicted a sooner than later Ice Age. Those who believed in a warmer Earth maintained it might soon be too warm for human survival. Those who predicted unpredictability? Well that was obvious, wasn't it?

Maybe that was part of his worry? Because he, because mankind in general, could not count on their experts anymore, he wanted to be better than that. He wanted to be reliable. He wanted to be a person that others could count on, and he wanted his office to be a source of healing in a hurting world. Wasn't that what all Christians are supposed to do? Weren't believers supposed to demonstrate their belief by healing and helping and guiding? The old stories about lighthouses and homes built upon rock and salt and light? Weren't they all about making the world a better place and making the people better people until Jesus returned or until His people were called home to heaven?

It was not easy being the Elder Director, but Jacob had never looked for easy, just for efficient and effective. And, he smiled a wry smile to himself, for success also. He wanted to be successful.

Maybe that should be his motto? He could have it put a little wooden plaque above the door, *Efficient, Effective, and Successful.* Jacob remembered a time when that plaque might have read *Hopeful,*

Faithful, and Fruitful. Were they the same mottos expressed in different ways? Or had he changed?

What a stupid question. Of course he had changed. Everybody changed. Jacob, Jacob, Jacob, he said his name silently to himself, get out of your head and get to work. Get to Alaska. Get there and get back and get your act together.

Chapter 24

The Teacher knew he was being followed. He had sensed it from the moment he had arrived in Sitka. Someone or something or maybe even both was tracking him, was following him with the intention of hurting him. He worried just a little about who or what it might be. These days he could deal with just about anything, if he knew what that anything was, but he liked to know with whom or with what he was dealing.

He had expected the Raven to return to him when he returned to the Southeast but so far that had not happened. He had seen many ravens, naturally, but they had not been the Raven, the Trickster, and that worried him. What exactly was that all about? Had the voices, the powers, realized his real motives? Had they begun to understand that it was dangerous for them to be understood? He wondered.

He wondered if he had underestimated the old ones and their old ways. Were there more serious control issues involved than he had previously anticipated? Had he tried too much too soon? There were many possibilities. There were so many possibilities that sometimes he gave himself a headache trying to keep track of them.

He was sure he would know, at least he would know better than he knew now, if he could see the Raven face to face again. As wily as the Trickster was reputed to be, as clever as he was in all the tales of his people, Randolph still believed a clever man could outwit him.

Randolph knew about hubris. He was not unaware of the legends and stories concerning folks who thought they were smarter than the spirits, more clever than the gods, wiser than the ancient ones. Ran the Man was not pretending to abilities or ambitions like that. He simply believed that the Raven, the Trickster, had a limited repertoire. One who studied his wiles and his ways could see patterns and make predictions based upon those patterns and avoid the foibles and the pitfalls that the less studious and cautious could not.

For a moment he smiled at his own reasoning. Ran the Man, proud of his lack of pride. That was something to laugh about. "What fools these mortals be," he murmured to himself. How long ago had Shakespeare written that? And how true was it still today? Very true, he decided. It was very true indeed.

Maybe it was even possible that he thought he was being followed because he wanted to be followed. He wanted to be worth following. He wanted to be feared, and respected. He wanted to be a problem for someone because he wanted to matter. Wasn't that what everyone wanted? To matter? How many philosophies and theologies and other ologies boiled down to that? People all wanted to matter.

Wasn't that what the main messages of all the world's religions were at their cores? Weren't they about reassurance? Weren't they about telling people that they were important, and that they were loved, and that – in the end – things would work out for their own good?

That was certainly how The Teacher played it. You are special. You are better. You have been chosen. You are loved and you will be admired. His young students wanted to hear this and they wanted to hear it not just from themselves and from each other, as important as that was, but they wanted to hear it from him too, someone older and wiser and more world-weary. From someone who had been around.

He had seen that so much during his own time as a student. Young learners and not so young learners alike wanted to be part of a continuum, of a tradition that helped anchor them in place and gave them, in turn, a place, a role as a link in that anchor's chain. It was so silly. There were so many old men quoting older men and trying to say new things even though they had nothing new to say and became frightened when they might. They didn't hunt their own game and butcher it. They didn't cook their own meals. They lived on regurgitated lessons. They worked with beloved teachers and their biggest goals were to become beloved teachers themselves.

Ran had heard that his cousin Bishop Bish had said that academia and macadamia were very alike because they both dealt with nuts, and that made him smile. Little Bear had always loved playing with words. Ran the Man preferred playing with people and people's minds and people's lives. He knew that about himself and he was fine with it; maybe he was even proud of it. And there he was, back to hubris again.

If he were being followed, how could he find the follower without being found himself? One of the first things he had learned growing up in Kake was that someone tracking the bear could very easily end up being tracked by the bear. The hunter could very easily become the hunted. Seeking to put meat upon the table was often an easy way to become meat.

His follower was either skilled or lucky. Ran had already tried the simple things like doubling back on his path as he walked in the town and the nearby woods. He had varied his routines and believed he had no regular habits that a watcher or a follower could discover, unless sitting in his room drinking coffee in the mornings and watching the news in the evenings counted as routines. He had no outside routines at least. Several evenings he had spent more money than he should have by eating in the restaurant across the street from his boardinghouse. The eatery had a rooftop patio and Ran sat there those long evenings until they closed at midnight, watching for his watcher, looking for his follower, but he saw nothing suspicious.

Perhaps that was what made him most suspicious, the fact that nothing suspicious was happening. After the incident at Muir, after Bishop returned to the Southeast, after the dispersal of his students and Kagi's reclamation of the sites he had borrowed from them, there should have been some repercussions, or at least some attempted repercussions. It was not right that no one seemed to care. At the very least, people should have been upset about the trespassing and the misappropriation of property.

That was why he watched the news every night. There had to be something there about the Muir incident. Someone had to care. Didn't they? Wouldn't they?

He had learned as a lad to be quiet in the forest when he was seeking game. He had learned to sit silently and to move silently and to listen. "Listen to the sounds of the animals," his father had told him many times. "And listen more when the sounds of the animals are stilled. When all of the animals are silent, something frightening is nearby."

So maybe Ran the Man was slightly frightened? Maybe it was too quiet indeed. He might be paranoid. He might be suffering from hubris. But there was no "might" about the silence. The world around him was just too still.

Chapter 25

"Lizzie and Laurie are selling the hardware," Diane greeted Bish as he came to the door.

"No, they are not." Bish laughed.

"Oh, yes they are. I heard it at the post office," Diane smiled even more.

"Oh, my, then it must be true," Bish laughed again.

"Are you suggesting the post office is not a reliable source of information?" Diane almost choked as she laughed too.

"Me?" Bish tried to look innocent. "Never, not me."

"Okay, just checking."

"Those hard weird sisters have been threatening to sell that place from the day they bought it," smiled Bishop Brewan. "I think they enjoy threatening to sell the store as much as they enjoy running the store, if that's possible."

"No, I don't think that is possible," Diane grinned. "That's got to be darn near impossible."

"So, what's the theory this time?"

Diane looked at her husband. "Theory? What do you mean by it.?"

"Oh, Laurie and Lizzie can't just be selling," he smiled. "There has to be some motivation for them to sell. Every time the rumor circulates the town that they are selling the store, there is a new theory about why they are selling the store. What's the reasoning this time? Did you hear?"

"As a matter of fact, I did," Diane nodded. "This time they are moving, moving to California."

"California?" Bish considered it a moment. "I have heard Seattle, and I have heard Portland, and I even heard Miami once. I believe it was Miami, though it might of been Houston, or someplace in the South." Bishop looked confused.

"What about this reason?" Diane watched her husband's face. "They met twin brothers on the Internet and are going to be married."

"I think I have to sit down for this one." For the first time in nearly a month Bish's knees were threatening to give out. "Tell me more," he poured himself some blucaf and settled back.

Most of the elements of the story were the same. The sisters were getting too old to run the store. The sisters were tired of being unappreciated. The weather was crappy. They weren't making enough money. People asked them questions and then ignored their advice. They were tired of playing nursemaids to hunters and handy men who had never met a tool they couldn't break.

"Have you seen their new sign?" Diane asked.

"I am afraid to ask, but I will. What's the new sign say?"

"Remember the one that said, 'If you break it, you bought it'?" Diane raised her eyebrows.

"Of course," Bishop nodded.

"Well, the new sign says, 'You bought it and you broke it, so you mucked yourself.'"

Bish loved the hard weird sisters. Kake would not be the same without them.

"How old do you think they really are?" Diane looked more serious now. "Are they in their 70s?"

"Well, since they have been around since Macbeth's time, I'd have to say they're closer to 700 years old." He tried to smile an innocent smile, but he could not keep a straight face.

"Someday, my love, you are going to mess up and call them the hard weird sisters, or make a Macbeth joke in front of them, or in the presence of someone who will repeat it to them." Diane looked serious.

"Never gonna happen, honey," Bish shook his head. "Never gonna happen."

"You know they run the bakery too, Hoppy. It's almost half of their business. Why don't you call them the 'half-baked sisters'?"

Secretly, Bish suspected that the sisters already knew he had a nickname for them. He had names for almost everyone, and since he had grown up in Kake, and since he'd had that habit as a boy too, no one would be surprised, probably. Sure, they would probably pretend to be surprised or offended even if he ever used it in front of them, but it would be an act. They knew, and he knew, and they knew that he knew, and he knew that they knew, but that was all part of living in a small town. Pretending that you knew everything and pretending that you knew nothing and playing your cards close to the vest. All things civil and courteous.

Bish laughed. "That would be mean. My Pennsylvania grandmother used to say, "If you can't say something nice about somebody, don't say anything at all.""

"How many of those sayings that you blame on your

Pennsylvania grandmother are really true?" Diane asked him now.

"On a good day, at least some of them," Bish grinned, "and on a bad day not so many."

"Do people around here understand that?"

"Oh, they understand it," Bish nodded his head, "even if they don't know it."

"I am not sure that makes sense," Diane looked at him over top of her glasses.

"It makes sense if you are from Kake," Bish replied.

"Speaking of being from Kake," Diane looked very serious now, "I found more in your Aunt Posie's journals."

Bish had been dreading this. Ever since Diane had found a brief reference to his family's interest in shamanism, he had been worried that she would find more. It was something he did not want to hear about, probably in the same way folks in the lower 48 did not want to hear rumors suggesting that their families had once owned slaves. They were facts that could not be ignored, even though you wished very much that they could. They were dark times.

"Okay, go ahead. Slowly."

"I'll tell you while you help me cook dinner."

Bish knew this was going to spoil his appetite, but he tried to smile anyway as he nodded and said, "Okay. That's a deal."

Diane had been reading about the Edgecombe Disaster in Aunt Posie's journal.

Chapter 26

No one was quite sure why it was called The New Northwest Passage when there had never really been an old Northwest Passage, at least not as long as records had been kept. It had been sought, many times, but no viable route through the region had been discovered. Now the march of The Melt had changed all of that. Shipping, inland shipping some called it, was flourishing. The Canadians loved it.

Canada and Southeast Alaska had a history of cooperation caused in part by the fact that the panhandle was geographically closer to Canada than it was to most of the Lower 48 and in part because the Alaskan Natives in both "nations" shared traditions, lifestyles, and ancestors. There were plenty of Tlingits to go around.

Bishop Bishop Brewan, half-Tlingit himself, thought that was the problem some days. There were plenty of Tlingit to go around, just as in Pittsburgh there were more than enough Pennsylvanians, and in Tucson so many Arizonians made daily life a challenge. Ministry would be so much easier if it weren't for so many sinners.

Diane laughed when he told her this. "Oh, yes, I know. Just the way education would be a great job if it weren't for all those students."

"And administrators?" He chuckled at her mock serious

expression.

"And school boards?"

"Don't forget the parents," he added.

"I wish I could. Argh." They both laughed then.

Strong-willed children grew up to be strong-willed adults. Diane and Bish knew their own kids were proof of that. Most of the time that was okay, perhaps even good. Most of the time. In a world where taking advantage of others and making money from the misfortunes and weaknesses of others was a common business model, knowing how to voice one's opinions and stand up for one's "rights" as a person were indispensable.

It did, however, make it more difficult some days to work with folks who had no intention of having their opinions and lifestyles changed—even if change meant improvement, or even enabled continuation. There was something in human nature that believed the phrase, regardless of in what language it was voiced, "We've always done it this way" was sacred.

"If it weren't for Tlingits and Haidas, and Tsimshians and Anglos, this would be a much easier job, Artie. They are all so stubborn."

"So, if the world was rid of sinners, life would be easier?"

"Yep, much easier. Nonexistent, mind you, but easier."

"Well, some say that may happen sooner than later."

Some did say that too. Sooner or later there would be no more room in Alaska for the Meltese Migration. Sooner or later in much of the world it would be too hot for human life to flourish. Sooner or later the rising seas and declining fresh water supplies would create panic and wars, and the disrupted growing seasons around the world would make the return of starving nations inevitable. People's actions and attitudes would have to change or they would perish. Some claimed that even with change it was going to be a very limited legacy for following generations. It was all "too little and too late."

Bish's Pennsylvania grandmother, Grandma Kaye, used to say, "Bloom where you're planted." It was her way of saying "Deal with it" in a grandma sort of way when Little Hoppy complained about the unfairnesses of life. Now that he was himself a grandparent, Bish passed on her wisdom by rephrasing the sentiment into "Make the most of your opportunities" and "Work with the materials and tools God gives you" when he counseled the grandkids.

Still, the basic message was "Deal with it." No one could change the past, but everybody had a shot at molding the future. Grandma Kaye had known it forty years ago and Bish knew it now in a way he imagined was more like her knowing than any ten-year-old kid could ever obtain.

Grandpa Ben had been dead seven or eight years, Bish wasn't quite sure, before his Alaskan grandson was born. Ben had never met Hoppy's mother, never been to the panhandle, and never guessed that any of his descendants would wander so far away from the Lawrence County farm where generations had been farmers, doctors, teachers, and lawyers, the only four careers really deemed acceptable by the Griffith family.

Bish had never understood the Welsh melancholy that seemed to cloud the faces and attitudes of Kaye and her brothers and sisters when they gathered for family holidays and wakes and marriages, but he was sure part of it had to do with their ability to drink huge amounts of whiskey at the slightest excuse and their inability to stop drinking even with the greatest motivation. Kaye's older brother, Ken, had died in an alcohol-related accident when he was barely thirty, and her twin sister Maye, had been in and out of rehab most of her adult life when she committed suicide before she turned forty.

Sometimes Bish wondered if getting a tendency toward alcoholism from one side of his family and an inability to handle much liquor at all from the other was his own particular manifestation of the "original sin" that scripture suggested accompanied folks from birth to the grave. People could be really mucked up almost from the "get go," Kaye's phrase for their earliest childhood. That was certain.

Would prejudices and stereotypes of "crazy Canucks" and "Yankee yahoos" gradually disappear as the New Northwest Passage increased interaction between the groups, or would they be reinforced by folks looking for validations of their biases? Bish wasn't sure, but betting on the tendency toward sin always seemed a safe bet. Sin was the biggest and baddest addiction of all, and it was there at birth, like the plague of "crack babies" in the Lower 48 and epidemic FAS children that cursed the Panhandle.

Certainly, Canadian and American businesses would utilize the NWP, and money would be made for a few people via the efforts and heartaches of many more, but would there be eternal consequences, benefits, or ramifications? Bish just wasn't sure how quickly the spiritual effects of the new trade route would appear. Would the powers that hated God and all those that God loved find increased opportunities for distraction, disruption, and destruction as people and ideas, deals and ideals, moved more quickly from culture to culture? Probably. What had ever been invented or discovered throughout humanity's history that the enemy didn't try to pervert? "Bloom where you're planted" could mean "Flourish here and now" or it could mean "You're stuck here until you die, so don't bother trying to advance."

For most of his life, Bishop Brewan had tried to "deal with" his problems, challenges, and dilemmas as they occurred, one at time or in bunches just like they did in everyone's life. For years as a pastor he had tried to deal with the problems and life challenges of his parishioners too. Marriages made and broken, children born and children buried, jobs won and lost, hearts stolen and then discarded. Sometimes that meant he could not, or at least did not, take the time and devote the energy to the hard parts of his own life. Sometimes it had been his excuse for drinking too.

Bish knew that Diane worried that he had not dealt fully with the loss of his parents at so young an age. They had been the most important people in his life and then they were gone. Posie and Martin and Kaye had tried to fill the hole in his heart with love and attention, and they had done a good job. Still, it was not the same, not the same as having two loving doting parents at your constant beck and call. Bish had been spoiled with too much coddling and attention and then he had been robbed of that kind of love, been forced to "detox cold turkey" Van would have said. All these memories mixed in Bish's mind as he listened to Diane read from Aunt Posie's journal.

Today Little Bear came to live with us. All rescue efforts have been abandoned as Sitka still sinks under the ashes of Edgecombe. We can only hope Daisy and Big Bear died quickly as the vapors flooded the town and did not suffer long. Authorities say most folks would have been dead before they realized what was happening.

Martin and I know Daisy wanted Little Bear to know the worlds of both his parents. We are resolved to keeping her wishes. His Grandma Kaye Griffith in Pennsylvania has agreed that he can spend summers there when he is ready. Or when we think it's time. Any other time is fine with her too. She says the farm is big and empty since Ben died.

I know they are all in Heaven now and Jesus has welcomed them with open arms. Their brief experiments with the old ways were the sins of youth and they settled down after the boy was born. They would want him to be a Christian and Martin and I will try to make sure he knows Jesus. The Bible says all things work out if we trust him, so that's what we're going to do. Martin says he will shoot that old raven if he catches him around the boy, and I think he means it too.

Diane stared at her husband. "Who was Martin threatening?"

"No," Bish shook his head. "Not a who, a what. Not raven the moiety like eagle, not the lovebirds. She is referring to a real raven."

"Are you certain?"

"Pretty much."

"So like Raven the Trickster?"

"I am afraid so."

"Like the bird on the boat that you told me about."

"Exactly like that. I am guessing."

"I see," said Diane but how could she? Bish wasn't sure he could see it himself. Had the battle he had always felt inside, the fight for his soul between good and evil, been an inherited struggle? Sure, it was all humanity's struggle since Adam and Eve mucked up in the Garden of Eden, but did he, Bish Brewan, have a personal family history with the combat that had been hidden from him?

He raised both of his eyebrows, "Is there more?"

"Just names of other Kake citizens killed at Sitka. Jackie's dad and others I don't know."

"No more about flirtations with malevolence?"

"Not here. But I will keep looking?"

"Good. And what else?" Her body language said there was more.

"I worry about our girls. Doesn't scripture say something about 'visiting the iniquity of the fathers on the children, on the third and the fourth generations'?"

Bish nodded, "But Ezekiel said 'The son will not bear the punishment for the father's iniquity, nor will the father bear the punishment for the son's iniquity; the righteousness of the righteous will be upon himself, and the wickedness of the wicked will be upon himself.'"

"We all make our own decisions." Now she looked relieved.

"Grandma Griffith liked to say, 'You made your own bed. Now lie in it.'"

"There were some strange women in your family," Diane shook her head as she stirred the soup that had begun to bubble on the stove.

Bish was tempted to say, "Bubble, bubble, toil and trouble," but decided against it.

Instead he pretended to be surprised. "What do you mean 'were'?" He might be getting older but he was still fast enough to duck the wooden spoon that she hurled at him.

Chapter 27

Bish hated the expression "Gone Native." It was an insult to Alaskan Natives and their heritages and a gross misrepresentation of what made his people a people. Still, he understood why Jacob Jaegar was using it now. To be fair, he had not had a haircut since returning from Pittsburgh, and he was wearing hoodies and ball caps more than he had before, but only around Kake, not on his rounds or to "official functions."

"What do you mean by that? 'Going native'?" He watched Jaegar's face on the screen carefully.

"You look too much like a street person. What happened to the old dapper Bishop?"

"I see. So Alaskan Natives look like bums or burnouts to you? Is that what you're saying?" Bish was in the mood to be angry. Angrier. He recognized it as an old habit from his drinking days. Frustration led him to drink and drink made him more frustrated and he drank more, and on and on ad infinitum.

The adverse effects of the Cantabuse had been bad enough and he still became nauseous thinking about what would happen if he drank, because he still had the leftover pills Van had given him, even though he'd told everyone he tossed them. He knew he would take them again if the temptation became irresistible and he believed he was going to drink. If it killed him, it killed him, and then he'd finally be done with it, and his family and friends would be free of his stupidity and weakness forever, and that might be a good thing.

Wow. What was happening? He'd never had problems before with SAD, the Seasonal Affective Disorder that plagued so many at this latitude when the sun disappeared and dim days ran together and isolation and nihilism rampaged through the streets and spirits of the people like demons determined to destroy all hints of hope and happiness for the people of the villages. Which was it now, cause or effect, that was operating here? Was depression making him angry or anger depressing him? Or was it both? Or something else?

"Bish Brewan. Don't even go there. You've known me too long to say that. I've earned better from you." Jacob Jaegar actually sounded hurt instead of angry in response to Brewan's accusation.

He was right and Bish knew he was right. He wanted to say he was sorry. He wanted to apologize. But at the same time he wanted to shout and shake his fist at the Elder Director, to scream, "You don't know. You don't know because you've never been here. You've never been me. You've never done what you take for granted I can do every day without concern or consequence. You expect me to be nonhuman or super-human or supra-human or something so much beyond what I can be. I can't be your Bishop and your investigator and your lecturer and your all in all all the time."

But he said none of this. Instead, he hung up on his old friend and boss and just sat and sobbed. He was still crying when Diane came home two hours later.

She looked at his red-rimmed eyes and the empty coffee pot on the kitchen counter. She had feared this was coming. Addictive personalities were addictive personalities.

"How much blucaf have you had today, Hoppy? Think about it. How much?"

"Six cups maybe."

"Two at breakfast and two at lunch?"

"Yes. And two or three in the middle. Or maybe four. It was a long morning and I was writing a lecture for Pittsburgh. And I kept falling asleep, so maybe five?"

"And how much are you supposed to drink while you are on the pills for your leg?"

"'Supposed to'?"

"Maximum? How much? Read the bottle."

It was on the coffee table next to his recliner. He read it. "Two cups. Maximum."

"Two cups of ordinary coffee. Maximum. And you drank maybe six or seven cups of blucaf, which is almost espresso?"

"Not really espresso. Sort of. I guess."

"You are a dumb mucker."

"I may owe Jaegar an apology."

"You are a double dumb mucker."

A trip to Juneau to his primary care physician confirmed that Diane was right. And wrong. And so was he. He might be suffering from a little Seasonal Affective Disorder, or he might need to cut back on the coffee, and probably a combination of the two was part of the problem, but the main issue was stress.

"Stress?" Diane had picked him up in a taxi and they were headed down to The Tsunami Terminal, Juneau's new Meltese restaurant, the first, Bish was pretty sure to actually use the word *Meltese* as if it were a heritage or ethnicity all to itself. Bish remembered the Angloamish places his wife had loved in Cleveland, Ohio and the Tlingfrench place in Sheldon. He was a bit frightened. Hopefully, no one would invent a meltmex cuisine or a franconese before he died. If they did, the food would probably kill him anyway.

"Sure. I have stress. Is that hard for you to believe?"

"More stress than before?"

"Before when?"

"Before like when we were raising two daughters and you had a little church in Monroeville and were working on your doctorate all at once?"

"Maybe not more now. Just different."

Different how?"

How could he explain it without upsetting or worrying her? It was more now because he could hear the ticking clock louder than he had ever before. He could see the pages of the calendar turning faster and faster. His muscles were softer and his joints hurt more. His eyes and ears were weaker and he tired more easily. Sometimes he grew short of breath and now the doctor said that he was "prediabetic" whatever the muck that was.

Studies had already suggested that lifespans since The Melt began were averaging seven years less for men and four for women. His generation would die younger than his parents' and his children would be lucky to reach their sixties. He didn't even want to think about the longevity of his grandchildren. *Shortgevity* was more like it. How could all that be stressful?

He had so much work to do before God called him home. Books to write and classes to teach and a whole strategy for EPIC's future in the Southeast were just a few chores he had remaining. Was that stressful? How could he explain it without worrying Diane?

"Different," he shrugged. "Just different different."

She sighed. Why did she bother? He was never going to change. And would she still love him if he did? Oh yes, she would.

Chapter 28

Winter, or the period of time previously known as winter, finally officially arrived in Kake with record high rainfalls and temperatures. Half of Molly Morgensterne's attending congregation wore shorts and flip flops to the Christmas Eve service, splashing their way up the hill to the old high school, laughing and singing Christmas carols and dancing. The rest dressed more traditionally and suffered and sweated for their efforts. Mrs. Diane Mercer Brewan thought it was great.

"Look how happy the children are," she whispered, "even though there's been almost no daylight for a month now. Just a few hours a day and most days they see some light but not the actual sun."

"Wow, Artie. That's got theology 101 material all over it. Our job as Christians is to show people some light until they actually see the Son, of God. I may steal that for my next lecture vid."

"If you do, give me credit," Diane squeezed her husband's arm and smiled. How many years had it been since they sat together on Christmas Eve? At least twenty? Maybe more. It had not been easy to convince EPIC's Bishop to Southeast Alaska to turn down requests to lead or assist in worship on this magical night, but her pleas and Jaegar's validation had won her husband over. She still wasn't sure why he hadn't fought the idea more.

Bish knew, but Diane hadn't directly asked, and it wasn't something he was ready to talk about, at least not yet. Sometimes saying something out loud made it more real than it was if you kept quiet, and he wasn't sure yet how real he wanted his thoughts or perceptions to be. For at least a decade now Bish had taught his seminary students the BPT theory of leadership, Barnabas and Paul and Timothy. The early Christian Barnabas had bravely volunteered to teach Paul while many others were still afraid Paul's Christianity was a hoax. Later, Paul had been willing to train Timothy when others were less patient. Everyone needs to be trained, Bish knew, and everyone needs to be willing to train. Traditions and beliefs have to be passed on from generation to generation, from leader to leader, if they are to survive and thrive.

There had been a time in his grandfather's era when the age of 60 had been heralded as the new 40. Bish, knew however, that those golden days were gone. In fact, he suspected, that math might be better reversed now. Soon some study would proclaim that 40 was the new 60. Halfway between the two, more or less, Bishop Bishop Brewan needed to find and train someone to do what he was doing now before he could no longer do it.

Part of this realization meant that Bish needed to spend more time in intentional monitoring and mentoring. It was great to be a sounding board for those seeking counsel and a listening ear to the laments of the local pastors, but it was not enough. It was also fine to be slowly honing in on the movements and methodologies of the enemy's forces in Southeast Alaska, but it was not a job to be left half done for whoever wore the burgundy vest after him. He needed to pick up the pace. He needed to admit to himself what Diane and Jacob Jaegar and, probably, most of the Elder Council already knew. He was getting old and in another decade would be too old, too old to be double Bishop anymore.

So, there was some pressure, even on this warm Christmas Eve as he listened to the warm rain falling on the roof and the warmly comforting words of Pastor Molly and the songs bouncing off the walls of the old classroom turned worship center in one of the nicest villages in the most beautiful place in God's great creation. There was some pressure, but there was more pleasure. There was more delight than fright on this holy night. He leaned over and kissed Diane on the cheek, and heard some of the children in the pews behind them giggle, and he chuckled too. Pastor Molly was so right. God was great and God was good.

Chapter 29

If Aunt Posie had still lived in Kake, her journals certainly would have recorded this winter as one of the strangest she had ever experienced. Weeks of warmth and rain alternated with weeks of drought and cold. Days that began with every indication of calmness devolved into afternoons of storm and nights of hail and ice. It had always been wise to dress in layers in Southeast Alaska because the weather could change quickly. But this was beyond all remembrances and certainly beyond any semblance of sanity now.

In Muir Pastor Brian Meade had opened up a soup kitchen in the church, using his culinary expertise to feed his flock physically now, even as he struggled to fill its spiritual appetites and needs. After eating there once, Bish decided he would be a regular customer if Pastor Meade ever opened a restaurant. That man could cook.

In Yakutat Suzie Taylor and her new beau were teaming up to do what pastor Taylor called Preventative Law Enforcement and Christian Education, or PLEACE. Their Wednesday evening classes at the church also included hot meals for many individuals who might otherwise have been cold and hungry. Yakutat's declining weather meant a declining economy too.

Pastor Patrick Murphy in Sheldon still struggled with the differences between doing what people wanted and what God wanted. The young guy had needs and wants hopelessly mixed together in his view of what made a church a church. Bishop Brewan dreaded going there to hear Murphy's sermons on Sundays. It didn't help either that Diane like to make these trips with him and drag Ronni and Van and Beatrice to those weird eateries she so enjoyed.

In Craig Elaine Johnson was a bigger mess than ever. Brewan was not sure, okay he was sure but he couldn't prove, that Pastor Johnson hadn't returned to her dragon tail marijuana past. If things did not change soon, he was going to ask Ketchikan's more experienced pastor to sign on as her official EPIC designated spiritual counselor.

Ketchikan, Petersburg, and Auke Bay were still blessed with pastors who could preach and teach, who listened and loved, who had servants' hearts, and who did not need much help from Brewan. He knew he should spend more time with them instead of punishing them with his lack of presence for their own capabilities and independence. However, until spring, that was probably not going to happen.

The isolation created by the distances and the geography of Southeast Alaska was something that most folks in the Lower 48 had never experienced and could not understand. For centuries it had made the entire state a sort of alien planet to the rest of the nation, a place exotic and intriguing, a desired destination for vacationers and an idealized home for those whose hearts marched to the beat of a different drummer. Since The Melt that isolation, coupled with the influx of the Melties, had intensified. Bishop Brewan did not approve of the Alaska for Alaskans movement, the AFA, but that did not mean that he did not understand it. Despite modern communications and conveniences, in many ways Alaska was as different from the Lower 48 as the early American colonies had been from Mother England.

Bish Brewan had lived long enough to understand that right and wrong were often abstract terms separated in theory much more easily than they were in real life. Sometimes people did wrong things for the right reasons. Sometimes they did the right things for the wrong reasons. Any consideration of sin needed to examine the motivations of the actors as well as the ramifications of the actions.

Unfortunately, people too easily found justifications, what they thought were good reasons, for doing bad things. Back in seminary, when Bish was a student, the classic example cited by his old professors was the number of young graduates who really, they convinced themselves, were "called" to ministries in Hawaii. Those old guy's stories were, of course, from before The Melt. Today, Southeast Alaska probably had more Hawaiians then Hawaii did.

Diane was headed to Tucson to visit the girls and the grandkids and Posie and Martin. Hopefully, she would get to see Violet also. Bish wanted to go along, but he knew he should remain in the Southeast. He did not want all of his pastors and all of their people to see him as someone who fled from the weather in this weirdly changing world. Still, his inner self whined, he wanted to go too. He laughed at his own childishness. Later, he could go later. And he would, later.

Strangely, somehow in a way that Bish could not understand, but in a way that made him smile every time he thought about it, Artie had formed some sort of strategic alliance with the sisters who ran the bakeshop and hardware store. Those two ladies, his wife told him as she packed, would make sure his pantry was well-stocked in her absence. They would also keep her well informed of any altered eating habits that they observed which might be leading Bish down the road to full-fledged Type II diabetes. He sighed. Women. What was a fellow to do?

"The hard weird sisters? You are leaving me to the double bubble toil and trouble duo?"

"You bet I am. And you had better behave. I will know."

"Oh dear. The things we do for love." They laughed together as he helped her pack.

Chapter 30

"The first time I ever drove in Mt. Washington," Bish was taping a vid for the seminary in Pittsburgh, "was on a dark rainy autumn night." Bish smiled at his own memory, wondering how many times he had told the story, and wondering too, why he had never recorded it before. He thought it was a good story.

"I came around a bend in the street and I hit the brakes. It loomed in front of me in the fog and I didn't know what to do. Was the street in front of me actually that steep? Or had I come upon a wall placed there by city maintenance to block off the street? I really couldn't tell.

"If I continued driving would the wheels of my car follow up that incline or would my headlights be smashed into the brick? For a moment I was afraid to do anything. Then I said a prayer, and I proceeded with caution."

Bish paused for a moment, hoping it would seem like a dramatic pause instead of a lapse of memory on the part of an old man, and then he continued. "That's the way it will be many times in your service to God. You come around the corner or around the bend in the road and you'll be faced by something that could either be an obstacle or a path to higher ground. And you will have to choose. You will have to choose. Will you turn around or will you proceed with prayer and caution?"

For himself, Bish Brewan knew, proceeding with prayer had never been much of a problem. Moving ahead with caution, however, was a different story. If his Grandma Kaye's maxim that "Only fools rush in where angels fear to tread" was valid, then Bish must have made the angels fearful many times in his life. So why was he so timid now? When he knew a confrontation with Ran the Man was inevitable, why did he dread the day of its coming?

Bish had asked himself this many times. He knew he was not afraid of his cousin. That would be silly. Was he afraid of the forces controlling Randolph? Of course he was. Who would not be? Powers and principalities were nothing to be trifled with. That, however, that was still not quite it.

Was he afraid of failure? Of course, he was. Wasn't fear of failure the one thing that made him always strive to excel? To succeed? Who was not afraid to fail? Only those who did not understand who they served and what the stakes were in this ungainly game they all played, the game they called life. Only a fool, indeed, would not be afraid of failure.

But yet, there was something else. Bishop Brewan had no doubt that one day he would stand before the Lord. He also had no doubt that when Judgment Day came he would be saved by the grace of his Lord Jesus Christ. He had been forgiven, was still being forgiven, and that forgiveness would find him an eternal home in Heaven. He was not worried about that. So, what did worry him?

He had a dread that on Judgment Day when God looked at him, when Jesus watched them standing there, that God would have a look on his face that said he was very disappointed in Bishop Bishop Brewan. He could have done so much more. He could've done so much better. He had such great potential, but he had wasted it. He had let his life trickle through his fingers and he never became the man that God created him to be, never the man God wanted him to be.

That was what he feared most, disappointing God. Wasn't that what sin was all about, disappointing God? Failing to be the wonderful creations that God intended them to be? Wasn't all sin about failure? It was not failure to try, not failure to succeed, just failure to be. Ontology, they called it in academics. Be. He wanted to be the man God wanted him to be. That was why he feared the competition coming with Ran the Man. He was afraid he would not be.

It was so much more important to be than to do, in this situation. Could he be for his cousin a representation, an embodiment, a message, that would persuade Ran the Man to follow a new and different path? How could he be an instrument of God's peace? How could he be an instrument of God's grace? How can you reach out to someone so fallen, so loss, so confused?

Bish knew that he needed to proceed with prayer and caution, not with fear and trembling. He knew he needed to pray more and he knew he needed to proceed more. But it certainly was not going to be easy. It certainly was not going to be fine. It certainly was going to be one of the hardest things he had ever done.

So where exactly now was Ran the Man? One of the advantages of being Bishop is that one has a sort of network, he told himself. He had called all the pastors in the Southeast, hoping someone might've heard a rumor, hoping someone might have seen Ran the Man, hoping someone knew someone who knew somebody else, but he still had no clue where Ran the Man was or what he was up to.

Was it a wall? Or was it just a steep incline? Most of the time, Bish did not believe in walls, at least walls without doors or windows. Most of the time he would find a way through or around any obstacle that kept him from doing what God was calling him to do. This time, however, he was not sure. Was he facing a steep uphill climb or was it really an impenetrable impassable wall?

When he thought about it, wasn't a wall the steepest uphill climb of all? He wasn't sure exactly why he had thought that. Was he telling himself that even walls could be climbed? Or was he telling himself the sometimes the climb is too much, the hike is too steep, the risk is too great? What exactly was going on?

Bish wrapped up the vid quickly, sending it back through

hyperspace to the seminary. It should be used tomorrow, who really cared? He was fulfilling the obligations that were part of his job. He was following the letter of the law. The spirit of the law was not as close to his heart as it should have been. Was he facing a wall, or a steep climb? Time would tell.

Chapter 31

Looking back someday scientists would probably realize that the term "permafrost" was a dangerous misnomer. It might have been better to call it the 'temporary frost" or "tempofrost," or something like that. Permafrost sounded too permanent, to unapproachable, too resilient. In reality the permafrost was not resilient at all. When The Melt progressed and the snow and ice were gone and the temperature began to climb, the permafrost began to unloose the secrets it had harbored for centuries.

How much carbon was stored in the permafrost? How quickly was it being released into the air? How serious, how intense, should concerns be regarding the permafrost's role in the irreversibility of the worldwide warming?

The ice and snow were obvious things. When snow melted everyone could see its absence, if absence could be seen. Everyone noticed when ice disappeared, even if all they noticed was the water left behind, the water that was flooded the world now. But human eyes could not see the carbon creeping out of its long stasis, the carbon collected in reflecting the sun's rays in ways and levels that the scientists had only begun to understand in the last decade. What would be the legacy of the permafrost that was not permanent at all? Would it be the end of humanity?

Bish felt sort of silly asking himself this question. He did not believe in the end of humanity. Oh sure, humanity's life on this earth might terminate. God might shut everything down again as He had done in the day of Noah, albeit in a different manner. But he believed, Bish believed, that the human soul was eternal, was not going to perish, people were not going to perish, in the sense of finality that so many associated with the word perish. The planet on the other hand? The Bible did talk about a new heaven and a new earth. There were indications that the old would pass away. Was the passing beginning now? Was the warming permafrost going to release germs and bacteria and viruses that people simply could not handle? Was the temperature going to rise so rapidly, rushing beyond that narrow range where most people could live, in just a few short years? He did not know. Bish Brewan did not know and he knew he did not know, and he wished that he simply cared just a little bit more.

His job and his calling were to be more interested in people's souls than in their comfort. He knew life was short and tumultuous and he never expected it to be any other way. Were the carbon gases loosened more and more each day into the sky going to help save souls? No, they would not.

Bish had done some research. For thousands of years the world's permafrost had acted as a sort of carbon sink, storing dead vegetation and animal matter and preventing, or at least slowing, its decay. This had prevented, or substantially slowed, the release of huge amounts of carbon into the atmosphere, slowing the greenhouse effect. Now those benefits were almost gone and that was dangerous.

The world was not only getting warmer, it was getting warmer faster as the atmosphere held in more of the sun's energy. The sky was getting hotter.

Not only was the sky getting hotter, it was getting less breathable. Methane gas was being released in quantities unimaginable to even the most pessimistic scientists of two generations ago. Asthma rates were skyrocketing. Shortness of breath was not just a problem for the old and infirm anymore. Children born prematurely had less likelihood of survival than any time since the 19th century. Any disease or injury that weakened the lungs could be fatal. People feared getting pneumonia as much now as they had 300 years ago.

The sky was getting hotter and the air was getting dangerous and the ground was falling apart too. In some regions of the old cold world permafrost had never been more than a meter thick. In other places, however, it had reached nearly a kilometer down into the ground. As The Melt continued the soil was deeply disturbed in many places. Sinkholes and landslides were no longer rarities, even in places once considered fairly stable. Building codes in Anchorage tried to take into consideration the disastrous potential for an increasing population living on a land increasingly susceptible to sinking beneath one's feet or one's car or one's home or place of business. The world was crumbling, literally.

Borrowed time. That's what Uncle Martin used to call it, borrowed time. When someone was very old, was very ill, or had escaped from an accident by some seemingly impossible turn of luck, Martin would say, "They are living on borrowed time." Now it seemed as if the whole world was living on borrowed time. The problem, of course, was the same for time as it was for anything else. When you borrowed things, you are expected to pay them back. The world had grown very old and very ill and in many ways had been very lucky to survive so long. Now, apparently, it was payback time. The bank wanted its money back. The planet was demanding that the huge debt mankind had run up for years be paid.

Bish shook his head and smiled, sitting in the drizzle on the deck at Posie's Perch. Someone, he could not remember who right now, had once told him that one of the scariest or meanest wishes one person could have for another was, "May you live in interesting times." Well, things certainly were interesting and they were probably going to get more and more interesting until that borrowed time ran out.

Chapter 32

Diane Mercer Brewan had known and loved Bish for over three decades, through thick and thin, in good times and in bad, for better and for worse, and she had never regretted marrying him, at least not for more than a few moments at a time, like any spouse did occasionally. If however, she had read Bish's Aunt Posie's journals thirty-five years ago, she might have run screaming in the opposite direction. Her husband Hoppy came from one messed up family.

She sighed as she closed the book she had been examining. She needed some coffee. Bish was sitting out in the rain, staring toward the sea, thinking who knew what thoughts? The worst of winter was over now and the sunshine was returning bit by bit. Before long it would be the Easter season. Could they not all use a resurrection?

Diane had stayed longer in Tucson than they had originally planned, and if she concentrated upon it perhaps she could feel just a little guilty about that, so most of the time she chose to concentrate on other things. Both of their daughters had married well, in the sense not of finances but of spiritual health and wealth. Their husbands were good men, and she and Bish had three delightful grandchildren. It would be wrong to be anything less than grateful, yet she still worried sometimes. Sometimes it seemed that the more people you loved the more people you had to worry about. And Diane Mercer Brewan did worry. The world was not a safe or happy place, not anymore, if it ever had been.

In her decades as an educator Diana had worked with all sorts of students, with children and adults, with the talented and the challenged, with the determined and the lazy, with the motivated and the unmotivated, and she had always found ways and reasons to hold her students close to her heart. This family of Bish's, she tapped the closed cover of the book on the dining room table, might have been the exception to the rule, if she had met them without first meeting her husband. They were crazy.

Diane knew "crazy" was not a politically correct term, nor was it very functional or useful. But crazy is what they were, crazy in an intense, obsessive, delusional sort of way. They really thought that they were different than other people.

She and Bish had always agreed that for the most part they did not want to behave or misbehave the way so many people of their generation did. They believed in working hard and playing hard and in making the hard decisions in life. They believed in love, tough love, and love that conquered all. They believed in focus and ferocious loyalty and family unity. They believed they were called to and could and must live up to a higher standard, a New Testament standard, than did so many of the people around them. But this was an action, a decision, a way of life. It did not make them better. It only made them behave better.

They both knew that on the inside they too were children of Adam and Eve. They had sin in their hearts, and no matter how hard they tried they could not improve themselves. Only through God and the long process of sanctification that lasted an entire lifetime could they be improved. They were not better than others, but they were forgiven, and they were expected to behave better than those still lost, those who did not know the grace and mercy of God's son.

Bish's ancestors, on the other hand, had actually seemed to think they were superior beings. Page after page of Aunt Posie's writings told stories of hubris and self-righteousness that had led Bish's ancestors down many paths to distraction. If Diane was the sort of woman who believed in curses, she could easily have believed that her husband came from a family that had been cursed for generations. How in the world had Bishop Bishop Brewan become such a normal man? It had to be grace. Grace and maybe the influence of such a good wife too? Wives were important. Diane closed her eyes and thought about the words she had just read.

Albert's first wife was the daughter of the old chief everyone called the Mountain Frog. His people lived in the hills and kept to themselves. They were kind to strangers but had nothing that encouraged others to join them as they lived and worked in a place where the fish were not plentiful and the winters were harsh. Mountain Frog was a wise leader and a peacemaker known for his gentle spirit and his powers of discernment.

He was a good man and a kind father but his daughter wanted to live in a wilder world. She was only 14 when she left the hills and the ways of her people, seeking to live like the white men and their bright women in the town of Juneau that the new owners of the land declared their capital.

Albert met her when she was 16 and he was 17, just finishing his studies at Sheldon Jackson. He dreamed of a life working in a fishery, the quiet life, but when he met her those dreams were destroyed. She had been studying too and the lessons she had learned were not good ones. Her body was her bait and Albert was hooked and reeled in before he knew he was even in the water.

Their marriage lasted less than 18 months and ended when she ran off to the lower 48 with a rancher from Montana. Albert followed her there, and was gone for three months before he returned, announcing, "She died." It was almost 5 years before he remarried, this time to a Tlingit girl from Kake who gave him three sons and two daughters who were the pride of his old age. My mother was the younger daughter. She taught me the songs I passed on from her father to my own children and the stories of Raven and how he stole the sun.

Diane opened her eyes, hearing Bish coming in off the deck. He hung his raincoat in the corner, letting it drip on the plastic rug there. "Wow," he smiled. "It's too wet even for me now."

"Hoppy," she looked at him and smiled sadly, "do you believe that people ignorant of history are really condemned to repeat it?"

"Yes, I do," he chuckled. "I also believe those fully aware of history are condemned to repeat it. Most of us only learn from our own mistakes, not from the lives of others."

"I've been reading more of Aunt Posie's journals, and they can be very depressing."

"I am sure of that," he stopped smiling now. "I am very very sure of that. Perhaps you should not read them?"

"Oh, probably you are right. But it's hard to stop."

"Yes, that's what all we addicts say." He moved into the kitchen to refill his cup of blucaf.

Diane watched him. He was right. Posie's words were sometimes like a bad drug, enticing and evil, enlightening and destructive, beckoning and bewildering and baleful. Perhaps she should read no more? And, perhaps, what she did read she should keep to herself. Secrets were not always bad, where they? Sometimes it was secrets that held people together, together with each other, and together in their own heads and hearts. Secrets let people pretend they were the people they wanted to be.

On the other hand, pretense could be a barrier to improvement, to reality, to the realization of how things really were versus how they could be. Diane took a deep breath, "Hoppy, is everyone in your family crazy?"

Her husband laughed, "Yes, they are. I thought you knew that by now."

Chapter 33

Pretty Pretty Girl a.k.a. Trixie a.k.a. Tricksy a.k.a. Bea was starting to act like a human. As winter turned into spring Beatrice's hostilities began to melt away and Ronni and Van began to believe, despite their past experiences, that this defensive little girl might grow into a wonderful young woman.

"God still works miracles, you know," Ronni smiled.

"Yes, he does indeed," Van agreed.

"But time alone will tell," Ronni had to add.

"Time is a blabbermouth. Time always tells."

The winter months had brought several "suitors," as Van liked to call them to embarrass Beatrice, to the shop again and again. Unfortunately, they were not all "suitable suitors." Between them, Ronni and Van scared away two thirds of them. Pretty Pretty Girl rejected a couple outright, and as Easter approached there were only four serious young men remaining.

Ronni laughed at her man when she heard him say "serious young men" and he had to join in.

"Oh my goodness. How old am I?"

"You sound pretty old." His wife laughed some more

"Just think how bad it will be when we have daughters," Van shook his head.

Ronni just chuckled, but something stirred inside her. It had been a long time since they had talked about having children, several years at least. With all the problems they shared and all their individual problems, they had spent their first years together agreeing that children might not be a good idea. So many things in this world seemed hereditary and neither thought they really wanted to pass on their problems to children who had no say in what genes they received.

They had briefly discussed adoption, knowing how many orphans there were in the world now, orphans from many places destroyed by The Melt and orphans sent with relatives to Alaska when their parents died or could only afford safe passage for their offspring but not for themselves. Ronni and Van were both still young and had good reputations now and had managed to stay clean long enough that adopting would not be that difficult for them, but for some reason they had just kept putting it off. Now Ronni wondered if subconsciously they had both hoped that God would work a miracle for them too and that someday they might be able to have a biological child.

She saw that Van was watching her closely, and she sensed that his thoughts were very similar to hers, but she wasn't ready right here and right now to pursue this topic. They were talking about Beatrice, a young lady that was here, that was here now and needed them in the here and now. In a few months maybe they could revisit the topic. In a few months when they both had more confidence in Trixie, when they both had more confidence in their own abilities to mentor someone younger and needier, that would be the time to talk. But for now it was still good to know that there might someday be a generation that would outlive them, a generation that make might carry some hope into the future and for the future.

"I remember Bishop Bish once said that he felt he could only give up on people when God gave up on him and God had promised he never would," Ronni smiled again.

"Never? That's even more than the biblical seventy times seven," Van sighed a fake exasperated sigh and held his head in his hands as if to keep the thoughts from exploding.

"I'm afraid it is indeed. For some folks it's a lot more," Ronni waggled her eyebrows knowingly.

"Right back at you, kid. Right back at you," her husband laughed.

In the next room Trixie was listening. She was not the girl she had been when she had come to stay with Ronni and Van, but she was not quite yet either the young lady that they hoped she was. She knew it was wrong to eavesdrop but she could not help herself. Knowledge was a weapon, a defensive weapon perhaps, but a weapon nonetheless. She needed to know everything she could know in order to protect herself. Whoever had said ignorance was bliss was ignorant. Only an asshole would believe that. And she was nobody's fool.

Sometimes Beatrice felt that there were two parts of her personality, the good side and the bad side. She remembered seeing a cartoon years ago in which a devil sat on one shoulder of the main character and an angel on the other, both whispering in the character's ears. Sometimes Beatrice felt like that. Sometimes she felt a voice telling her to grow up to be the fine young lady that these interesting men that came to see her every week thought she could be. Sometimes the voices told her that Ronni and Van were worse than any parents ever could be, that they used her and abused her by making her work in the shop, even though no one had forced her to do it. Still, it was expected, said the voices, expected and who knew what would happen if she did not meet their expectations? It might be better not to know.

Sometimes she felt torn into little pieces, one part Beatrice and one part Trixie and one part Tricksy and one part Pretty Pretty Girl. It gave her a headache trying to determine who she really was. Maybe she was not any of these people, and maybe she was all of them, and maybe she was in flux, lost someplace wandering from personality to personality and character to character.

In flux? Was that even possible or was that just something she had seen on television? Sometimes she wasn't sure what was real and what wasn't real. Sometimes her old life seemed like a dream, a nightmare that she had awakened from and thought for a time was real but understood now wasn't.

Still, she knew it was real. Several times in the last month while walking through Sheldon she had sensed in her peripheral vision the presence of The Teacher and turned, fearing what she would see, but he was never there. He was never there but he was always there, and as the months had passed she understood more fully what would've happened if the interfering little Bishop had not arrived to rescue her. She would awaken sometimes at night, crying, shaking, and Ronni would come in and hold her and whisper to her, trying to calm her, until one or both of them fell asleep.

If she hadn't seen the newspaper articles it might have been better. But she had seen them. In the last few months she'd spent more time in the library than she had in all the years of her life before. She wanted to understand poetry so she did not seem like Stupid Stupid Girl, the girl her parents had always told her that she was, when she met with this first suitor, the first in appearing at least, and maybe, she realized now, the first in her heart still.

But in the library there were always newspapers, too many newspapers for the small amount of local news, so old stories were rehashed at the slightest excuse. A missing girl from the ferry traveling toward Yakutat had reinvigorated interest in the incidents of the past several years, providing an excuse for reporters to speculate on the possibility that a serial killer still roamed the Southeast.

As much as she did not want to believe it, Beatrice now had to consider the possibility that James Aaron had been right. Teacher might be a maniac, a dangerous dangerous man interested only in himself and his own appetites. James had not said all of that, but she had heard it in his voice, in his tone, and she had seen it in the eyes of the Bishop. Ronni and Van never pushed her too hard, never were impolite or demanding about the events of her past, but she could tell that they too worried about her, about her past and about her future. As much as she still would have denied it, they felt like family now, big sister Ronni and older brother Van, her two crazy siblings. Most of the time it was a good feeling.

So why was she listening now? She was listening because she hadn't listened before so many times when she needed to, and she had promised herself that she would always listen now instead of being caught ignorant and unaware. Her poetry pal Charlie had taught her the importance of words, not just any words but the right words for the right occasions and the best words for the best sentences and one of the first things he had explained to her was the difference between being stupid and being ignorant. She had never been stupid, but she had been ignorant and she never intended to let that be part of her again.

So she was listening. In the voices of this new brother and sister of hers she heard hope and fear, and she heard joy and sorrow all mingled together. Ronni and Van had suffered fear and loss but they still had hoped, and maybe that meant she could too.

In the meantime she would keep listening, keep evaluating, keep making what her poet pal called "contingency plans." Escape routes was what she would've said and that thought made her feel bad about herself for a moment. Why was she thinking that she needed to escape? From what did she need to escape? She was in a place now that she would have run to, not from, at any other point in her life. What was wrong with her? Was this what Ronni and Van were talking about when they talked about sin?

She moved her ear away from the wall and sat on the edge of her bed, fighting back the tears that trickled down her pale cheeks. For the first time in her life Beatrice Nelson realized she might be a sinner.

Chapter 34

Briggs and the Boss met for lunch at the Boss' favorite café. The food was terrible and the wait staff was surly. Briggs was certain everyone in the kitchen had a criminal background. Most of the other customers looked shady, dangerous at best, homicidal at worst. No wonder the Boss loved the place.

"Are you fully adapted now?" The Boss raised his eyebrows and tilted his head with the question, wearing that stereotypical quizzical look Briggs knew the boss thought was so perfectly human. "Does everything work?"

"Oh yes, it's all fine."

"But does everything work?" The Boss said it emphasizing the word everything in a way that left no room for misinterpretation.

"Everything. Yes, everything." Briggs chuckled a chuckle to match the Boss' own. "At least it did last night."

"And has our little secretary figured out who you really are yet?"

"No, Boss. She has not."

"Are you sure? Are you really sure?"

"Why do you ask? You told her?" Briggs did his best not to

sound angry. But that would be like the Boss. He loved to play them one against the other. He could never resist that, even when it meant disharmony and disunity among the ranks. It was part of who he was, part of his nature to keep things stirred up all the time, to keep them on the edge, on their toes. It was his old modus operandi and it was very annoying.

Of course Briggs did his best to hide this. This was not something you let the Boss know, ever. Because "ever" would mean just once and that would be it. The real Briggs, the old Briggs knew this now, too late, and the new Briggs had no intention of meeting a fate like that.

"No, I did not tell her. Of course not." The Boss smiled, "How is your sandwich?"

"It's terrible."

"Yes, isn't that wonderful?"

Briggs laughed because there was nothing else he could do. The Boss laughed louder, chewing and chortling at the same time, looking for a moment more like himself than the man he pretended to be. Briggs hoped there were no photographers anyplace near.

The Boss was done playing now so he came to the point of their meeting. "I want you to send some help to the wolf."

"Some help? How much help?"

"Exactly. I knew you would understand, Briggsy. How much help indeed?"

"Wolf will not like that at all. He has a history with them you know?"

The Boss laughed even harder, almost choking on his sandwich. "Of course I know. But that's 'Nada' problem, "'Nada' problem for me at least."

They both laughed now, loud enough that they did draw the

attention of the other customers, but as seasoned and experienced as the regular customers looked, criminals all, they recognized in the two well-dressed men a level of danger that none of them was stupid enough to confront. Everyone pretended they heard no laughter at all.

Chapter 35

Muck was getting tired of that stupid dog, or wolf, or whatever he thought he was. On his own he would've stopped following Teacher halfway through the winter. Teacher had no hold on him now, so why should he care what that old man did? By following him around wasn't he allowing the man to still control him, whether he knew it or not? But the Wolf insisted. The Wolf demanded. The Wolf just might have to go.

Washing dishes was not a job Muck had expected he'd enjoy. It was menial and boring. It was mind-numbing and repetitive. Somehow, though, it was degrading and uplifting simultaneously.

Each day as he scrubbed away the debris of meals from the restaurant's plates, Muck could feel parts of himself being washed away too. He was in a place now in his head much better than where he had been six months before. Now he would never have called himself Muck, but because so many others did he kept the name. It was too much work to explain it to anyone.

Nada Dogg did not like this. Muck could tell. Sometimes when he was thinking about life, not what it had been but what it could be, he heard Nada growling softly, almost like an old man muttering under his breath. If he looked at him or tried to hush him, Nada seemed to be asleep and dreaming about whatever dogs dreamed about. He thought he was fooling Muck but he wasn't.

Nada Dogg was pretending he was not a Nada, but Muck knew better. When he'd chosen to not ambush the Teacher that evening months ago, he'd felt the anger and the frustration in Nada Dogg. The mutt had not spoken to him since then. He would growl or bark and whimper and whine, but he didn't speak anymore.

At first Muck had tried to convince him to talk again. "I know you can talk," he chided the dog. "And I know you're not really a wolf, or at least not only a wolf." He repeated it at least four or five times a day but Nada did not respond. After a while Muck stopped trying, but he did not stop believing, did not stop knowing. Those voices that spoke to him spoke to Nada too, and he knew they had not gone away. They might be in hiding, pretending to not be around, but they were there. They were always there. Now they were just biding their time, waiting for something, plotting and planning, he suspected, determining how to get him to do what they wanted him to do.

That had been the problem with Teacher, well at least part of the problem. Teacher had always thought that he could control the voices more than they could control him. Muck himself had thought that for a while, but in the last few months he had begun to realize that there was no negotiating with the voices. They pretended they wanted to compromise. They pretended he could have what he wanted and still do what they wanted, but he knew better now.

He wasn't quite sure how he knew, but he knew better now. He tried to think about this realization. Where had this knowledge come from? Beside him Nada growled again.

"Shut up, dog," Muck smirked. "Don't try to distract me. I know your old tricks."

He was going to have to get rid of this wolf, this haven for the voices. He was going to have to get rid of the dog, but he would have to be very careful because the dog might be planning to get rid of him too. Muck was not as stupid as they all thought he was. He knew they were trying to use him to get rid of Teacher even though they could have done it themselves. Nada could have crept off in the night and tracked down Teacher. A quick leap and a closing of his teeth around the man's throat and that would be it. No more Teacher.

But that was not what they wanted, those voices that lived inside Nada. They wanted Muck to do the job. They wanted him to be involved, to be the actor who took down the Teacher. Muck was not sure why this was what they wanted, but every day he became more and more sure that he did not want it if they did.

Teacher had never understood that. He had thought he could compromise with the voices. He thought he could find an avenue, a path, a course of action that pleased the voices and got him his own way too. For a brief time Muck had thought this way also. But he had figured out that he was wrong.

"Figured out" might not be exactly accurate. Had he figured it out? Or had someone or something told him? This was a problem he had been dealing with for several weeks now. Why had he come to the realization that there was no negotiation with the voices? Teacher was a smart man, but he had thought he could control the voices.

Teacher had never told him that, but he knew. He could see it in the man's actions, and the way he thought he used the voices with the girls. He never saw that the voices were using him and his sickness, his need for the girls, to capture him and keep him under their control. The voices were not stupid, certainly smarter than Teacher and certainly smarter than Muck too, but Muck knew this, and that made a difference.

Lots of things were bigger than, faster and smarter than people, but that did not mean that you had to let them win. Sometimes it meant you just avoided playing their game. Only an idiot would attempt to wrestle a grizzly bear. Only a fool would try to outswim a salmon. Only an asshole would try to make a deal with the devil.

And there it was. The devil. This was the first time he had said it. Teacher had always called them primordial forces, or "the voices our ancestors knew." He had said very little of them to Muck after he had decided that Muck was not a worthy disciple. But before then he had said enough to convince the lad that he really did hear things, at least in his head.

When Muck started to hear them himself he had taken it as an indication that he was a worthy disciple of the teacher. Teacher simply had not understood that. In time, Muck had thought, he would. But that time had never come and now Muck knew it never would, and that was fine also. If there was one thing he now knew he did not want to become it was the Teacher. He certainly did not want to have someone tracking him down with a Nada Dogg.

So. That was it. The devil? A force of and for evil. If that was what he was dealing with, if he wasn't just being silly and melodramatic here, he really did have to get away from Nada Dogg. And the dog, the wolf, might actually have begun to sense this before he understood it himself. Maybe that was another reason he had stopped talking?

How does one get rid of a devil dog? He laughed. "It's Nada easy thing to do."

Chapter 36

After so many years of teaching, after so many decades of teaching was more like it, it became difficult to come up with new images, new ways to explain things, but Bishop Brewan never gave up trying. Today he was working on his "grizzly bear" analogy.

"Imagine a man walking down the streets of Anchorage with a grizzly bear on a leash. People see him coming and they get out of the way. Children scream and run. Everyone who sees him understands that he is insane and they want nothing to do with him. This may frustrate him and alienate him. He may feel so isolated and alone that he wishes the bear would just die, but he does not let go of the leash. He keeps walking down the streets, down the same streets day after day seeing the same results.

"Children screaming. People running. Fewer and fewer wanting anything to do with him as time progresses.

"So he begins to feel more isolated and alone or he begins to feel powerful. He starts to relish the reactions, the fears, of those he meets. He is a big man. He has power and he can control others. After a while he begins to like the control, the power, and those things are what he starts to become. He no longer is who he was but instead he is control. He is power.

"He gets dumber and bolder and more wicked with each passing day, with each screaming child, with each running person. Once he was simply an idiot with a bear on a leash but now he is an invader. He is a person above the law, a person who does not need to pay attention to the petty rules and lives of ordinary people. He is a force unto himself.

"But, somehow inexplicably, he has forgotten that he is a man with a grizzly bear on a leash. He has forgotten that sooner or later that grizzly bear will turn around. That grizzly bear will see the leash. That grizzly bear will see the man. And then the real trouble for him will begin."

Bish played it back and nodded as he listened. It would do. They would understand, at least he hoped so. How much more simple could he make it?

Slowly, like a man awakening after an unexpected afternoon nap, Bishop realized he was hearing an unexplained sound. A light tapping sound, like someone knocking but wanting only the homeowner and not the neighbors to hear the sound, came from outside the window, out on the deck. Bish stood up and walked quietly to the sliding door. He held his breath and stood as motionless as he could. Five feet from him on the corner of the deck railing an eagle was perched, certainly the largest eagle he had ever seen. Bish's old legs began to tremble.

He had heard the story by now, certainly everyone in the Southeast had heard the story, the tale of the little girl and the big bird. Diane had related it to him less than a week after it occurred, sitting at their table with tears running down her face. He had tried to show no emotion then but now he could not control himself. His eyes were wet and it was hard to breathe. He was trembling all over, shaking so hard he could barely stand.

And now the bird turned and looked at him. It tilted his head first to one side and then to the other. It seemed to nod at him. Once. Twice. Three times. And then it stretched its body from the tip of its tail to the top of its head, and it spread its wings, showing a wingspan of at least ten feet, definitely the biggest eagle Bish had ever seen. And now it tilted back its head and it uttered a sound that hurt his ears, a screech and a call that made his body shake even more, and then with a quick flap of its wings it rose into the air and soared out of sight faster than any eagle should be able to fly.

Why did he not use his cane the way he should? He needed it now. Bishop Bishop Brewan held on to the door frame with one hand and reached over to the umbrella stand that sat on the plastic rug inside the door. He took two steps until he was at the umbrella stand. Then he could reach his chair. Holding onto it, he moved his body into it and sat.

He sat and he sobbed. Great gasps of air filled his lungs and his chest hurt. He sniffled and swallowed. His eyes ached and his ears were ringing. It was too much. It was too much. Too much wonder and too much grace and too much for any person to bear. He cried and cried and cried. God had just told him that God was not done with Bish Brewan yet.

Chapter 37

Diane Mercer Brewan moved a kitchen stool next to her husband's recliner. She still wore her light rain slicker and her wellies, her "Sitka slippers." She sat down and took his big right hand in both of her hands, and she looked straight into his eyes and she said, "I am so sorry, Hoppy. I am so sorry."

"Why?" Bishop Brewan's eyes were still red. He had blown his nose and wiped his eyes so many times in the last hour that they were sore. He knew he probably looked tired and he knew Diane would recognize that he was troubled, but how many times had she seen that before? Why would she be troubled herself now?

"Why, Artie? What do you have to be sorry about?"

"I am sorry I said that your family was crazy. And I think I am crazy too, my love."

"Ha ha, no," Bish shook his head and laughed. "Believe me, you are not the crazy one in this house."

Diane took a breath. She swallowed and then took another. Looking him straight in the eye, she asked, "Then why on my way home from the hard weird sisters did I think I saw your cousin Randolph on the beach walking a grizzly bear on a leash?"

Diane thought she might have to call 911. Her husband laughed and cried and sobbed and laughed more. He pounded the arms of his chair calling out "Yes, yes. You are crazy. I am crazy. The whole world is crazy. Don't you love it? Isn't it great?"

Diane didn't know whether she should be offended or astounded, but she was a bit of both. She wanted to be angry. He was laughing at her. But it was contagious and soon she was laughing too. They both stood from the chairs at the same time to wrap their arms around each other and hugged, and the tears ran down their faces and down the backs of their best friend, their lover, their helpmate, the one that God had given them to spend their life with. And they laughed and they cried. They laughed and cried more and harder than they ever had before.

Bish played the Pittsburgh tape for her and she became so still he was worried for a moment she was having a stroke. And then he told her about the Eagle and she became more still than still.

Standing in front of him she took both his hands in hers now and she bowed her head and he bowed hers and they prayed.

"Lord," Diane began, "what in the world are you doing? Are you trying to kill us?"

"Oh Lord, indeed what are you doing?" Bish echoed her words.

"We don't know what in the world you are doing." Diane said it again. "And we are terrified."

"Yes," her husband agreed, "we are terrified and we're honored and we're frightened. Thank you, Lord. Thank you."

They spent most of the evening talking about what it meant or about what it could mean because neither really had any idea what it meant. The only thing they knew was that something big had happened and that something bigger was coming. They were going to need to remember that God was in charge, that God was in control, and that nothing is impossible with God.

It had not been Randolph on the beach. They were sure of that. It was simply God reminding them that they worked for Him, that they were His children, that despite The Melt and despite their growing age and despite the mess that the world seemed to be in, God was still in control, God still loved his people and wanted the best for them and would act on their behalf as He saw fit. Not as the world wanted. Not as they hoped. But as He saw fit.

Diane wished she had seen the Eagle and Bish wished that he had seen the bear on the leash, but they both believed the other. And they both believed God had shown them what they had needed to see. Maybe they didn't understand it now and maybe they wouldn't truly understand it this side of Heaven, but they did not need to understand. God understood them. And God knew. God knew everything.

"I guess we both passed our stress tests for this year," Bish smiled at Diane. "Won't our doctors be pleased?"

"Sure." Let's call them up and tell them and see how fast they lock us up." Diane began to laugh again and Bishop joined her. Again they laughed until the tears ran down the cheeks. And then in the two recliners, side-by-side, his left hand in her right, they watched the long Kake sunset and they fell asleep together.

Chapter 38

Sitka, Alaska had never been a large town. Even before the Edgecombe Disaster people in the Lower 48 would have laughed at the idea of calling it a city. Now it was even smaller. How that stupid kid, James Aaron, could have expected to stalk him without being caught was something Ran the Man could not fathom.

The only reason he had not already confronted that punk kid was the wolf. The boy could pretend it was a dog but it was a wolf. The boy could pretend the creature was his pet too, but Randolph knew better. That animal might belong to someone, but it did not belong to stupid James Aaron.

Ran the Man was not exactly sure if he had been able to see auras his entire life or not. When he was in junior high school they had tested his eyes, looking for a retinal tear after he described bright flashes of light that seemed to come from nowhere and returned to nowhere without cause or warning. One doctor had suggested pre-migraine syndrome and another had wanted to fit him with special bifocal glasses, suggesting that his two eyes sent disparate signals to his brain. He had been in his early thirties before he learned to control what he saw.

Even now he was not sure that "control" was the right word. It might be more accurate to say that he had learned to focus on some things and ignore others. He could shut out the distractions the way a person living in the city in an apartment near the train track eventually stops hearing the trains and only notices when they are off schedule or stopped. The auras were there all the time but he did not look at them all the time. He only noticed them if they were unusual.

That was the problem with the wolf. The old ones had believed that animals had spirits too, like people did, but ordinary animals did not have auras. This was something that most eyes did not see and most brains did not understand, but Ran saw it and he understood.

People had auras and animals did not. Most of the time. So whenever an animal had an aura Ran paid close attention. It'd been that way with the Raven. Even before it had spoken to him and started flying nearby whenever he was out and about, Ran had noticed the Raven because of its aura. There was something different about that bird.

There was something different about stupid James Aaron's wolf too. It had an aura. A darkly bright aura that suggested something much bigger than the wolf itself, the sort of size and shape that Ran would have expected from a 300 pound man who drank too much and hated society and all its rules. Whoa. Now who was internalizing what?

Ran the Man had heard a few of his students talking about auras, and they always sounded crazy, and he was glad that he never said much about his ability. He never said much, but that did not mean that he did not see it as an ability, as a gift, as something that helped him stand above the others, an indication that he was special.

Gifts were meant to be used, he always figured, not left unopened at the party. Now he would rely on a gift and be cautious when dealing with the stupid boy and his special wolf.

Ran had decided to do what anyone fearful of being followed should never do. He'd developed and then displayed a set routine. He'd left and returned to his apartment the same way, following the same route, every day. He ate the same meals at the same places. He shopped at the same grocery store and washed his clothes at the same laundry. Every day. Week after week. Into the months that the weeks became. Ran the Man became predictable.

Predictability became his companion. Predictability was his friend. And after stupid James Aaron had grasped the predictability and had counted on it, that predictability would become a weapon that destroyed James Aaron. Ran the Man smiled, yes, predictability would mean the end of that stupid stupid boy.

Naturally he did not do it all at once. He buried the routine a little at first and less and less as time progressed, letting it not be instantly a routine, letting it instead gradually become a routine. He wasn't sure how long the boy and his wolf had followed him before he had spotted them but he suspected it was less than a week, maybe two at the most? Once he knew they were on his trail he had gradually made the trail easier and easier to follow, gradually lolling James Aaron into the sense of complacency that would end his nuisance, that would end him and his stupid pet wolf.

For a while he had feared that the wolf had caught on and warned the boy. The dubious duo was being cautious when there was no obvious reason for caution, but it turned out they were just slower than he had expected. In the last few weeks, thank goodness, it had become obvious that his "routines" had been observed and had been considered normal and real.

Only a fortnight ago he had seen the duo following him one block from his hideout and then not again until he was four blocks away, passing through an alley that was not in a straight line on his path, an alley you would only use if you were trying to be cautious, an alley they would not have accidentally encountered him in. And then a block from the restaurant where he ate on Thursdays he'd seen them again. They had not followed him. Instead they had assumed his normal path and had checked at certain points and certain times to make sure he was on schedule. And he was. He chuckled to himself, yes, he was predictable and wasn't that wonderful? What a great tool predictability was going to be for him.

Chapter 39

Bishop Bishop Brewan was not a happy camper. Why had that idiot agreed to let the AFA meet in the church? Every time Bish began to think that Pastor Patrick had begun to get a handle on the job he did something stupid like this. Pennsylvania Grandma Kaye would have called it "Taking two steps forward and one step back." This Alaska for Alaskans thing was more like one step forward and two steps back. There was enough trouble in the world these days with all the repercussions of The Melt. Nobody needed for the planet's biggest economy to get bushwhacked by a second civil war.

How many thousands of years did people need to be told that "a house divided against itself cannot stand"? Sometimes humanity seemed like a race of non-learners instead of simply a race of slow learners. And today Bish Brewan was not certain that Pastor Patrick might not be the poster child for non-learners. He sighed and took a long drink from his coffee cup.

One of the long-standing policies of the EPIC church was that clergymen were not supposed to get involved in politics, either local, regional or national. It was EPIC's understanding that when Jesus talked about rendering to Caesar what belonged to Caesar and rendering to God what belonged to God he was talking about more than money. Christians should not be distracted from their mission to spread the good news of the gospel of Jesus Christ by getting overly involved in the shenanigans of politics. That was Caesar's world, the world of power and intrigue, of control and of, well, mainly of control.

Politics is about people wanting to push around other people. No matter what mask it wore, it was still about people having their own agendas and wanting their own ways. Sometimes they actually believed they knew what was better for the world than the people of the world, the common folks, "the masses," as they had once been called, knew. And sometimes they did. But many times those differing levels of knowing were also because of politics.

When his own mother Daisy and her sisters had been children the great national education scandal, Edugate, had been in the news for months. When the Pittsburgh Post Herald had broken the story about the half-century long plot to undermine American education, some had feared there would be a revolution. Anyone with half a brain had known that governments can more easily control uneducated populations, ignorant people, than they can manipulate the well-informed. Few, however, had realized that all the policies mandating more tests and lowered teacher credentials and less local control had been intentionally implemented to guarantee that America's youth had less and less time every year to learn the essentials that they would need to function as citizens of a modern democracy. It was the old wolf in sheep's clothing tactic.

During that time, as the separation between the upper and lower classes had widened and the middle class had become nearly nonexistent, cyber schools and alternative schools and homeschooling had all been pushed by special interest groups whose real main interest was in keeping the nation's population too stupid and too distracted to realize that the United States was becoming a country crowded with people who knew much less than did the small group at the top that was determined to maintain and even increase its control of the rest of the population.

Free public education, a good free public education that had once been the envy of the world, had been almost eliminated by the time the evil endeavor called Edugate had been discovered and revealed to the public. After that, anyone really trusting politics and politicians, anyone not understanding the corruptive and corrosive qualities of power, was not simply stupid or ignorant. They were willfully stupid and ignorant. Why anyone would ever choose to give up their own freedoms, their own decisions, their own dreams and desires and directions, was something Bish still did not understand. Childhood was an essential part of being a person, but the children were supposed to eventually grow up.

Was Pastor Patrick Murphy ever going to grow up? Did he not understand that the Alaska for Alaskans movement was not really a grassroots attempt to gain rights and benefits for the people of America's forty-ninth state? How could he not see what the anti-Meltese movement was going to do to the entire northern hemisphere? The ancient grumble "we were here first" had always been ridiculous. Change and migration were part of the human condition. Circumstances changed and people moved and populations melded. That's how life worked.

Back in Pennsylvania one of the greatest obstacles that the church faced was the un-vocalized cry "We've never done it this way before." It kept churches small and Christians isolated from each other. It wasted money on redundant buildings and missions and pastoral salaries. The enemy understood well the divide and conquer strategy. The devil knew that houses divided against themselves did indeed fall.

Bish sighed again. He would go to the meeting and he would watch and he would listen. He would do his best, however, to not say a word. He was here to observe. It would be a great place to put faces on the forces of those who did not want mankind to successfully deal with the worldwide crisis that was The Melt. Representatives of Christ needed to be there because the other army would certainly have its soldiers on site.

Bish smiled as he thought about Grandma Kaye's favorite dishwashing hymn so many years ago in that big old Pennsylvania farmhouse. How did it go? Onward Christian soldiers? Marching as to war? As a child he had liked the song, but later he had rejected it as too militaristic. Even later, now, he had returned to it, understanding that life really was about a long battle, a long struggle, a war between one who wanted the best for all of His children and one wanted the worst for those children and their Creator.

At least this trip would give Bishop a chance to see Ronni and Van and Beatrice too. Bish was sure there would be interesting events going on in that house. He was so proud of Ronni and Van for their hospitality and generosity toward Beatrice. Pretty Pretty Girl was not an easy young lady to put up with, Bish was sure. But they certainly were hanging in there. Good for them. He smiled. It made his heart glad.

Chapter 40

Jacob Jaegar, Elder Director of the Ecumenical Partners in Christ church, arrived in Juneau, Alaska early Monday morning. He had flown from Pittsburgh to Chicago and then from Chicago to Seattle. After staying overnight in Seattle, he'd flown to Ketchikan and then on to Juneau where he was meeting Bishop Brewan, his host and guide on his first trip to Southeast Alaska. Jacob Jaegar was a bit excited.

Elder Director Jaegar had not been in the field that much in the last decade, and he realized now that he missed it. He loved his desk, really he did, but this...? This was what it was all about. Being in the trenches, in the field, among people, with the sheep of the flock God had given him, more, had *entrusted* him with. It felt good. Somehow, he felt at home here in Alaska, even though he had never been in this place before. It was going to be a good trip.

Outside Juneau Airport it was raining, raining the way Bishop Brewan had told him it always rained in the Southeast, raining like Seattle used to rain, only three times as much, gallons, waterfalls coming down from the sky, looking like they would last forever. Jacob Jaegar smiled to himself. Nothing lasts forever, he reminded himself, absolutely nothing.

His plane had actually landed early. It was not scheduled to arrive for another fifteen minutes. This was great. It gave him time to look around the airport, to grab a sandwich at the snack bar, and a cup of coffee. He stretched his legs, walking along the left wing of the terminal where all the private little airlines had their counters. He was amazed to discover seven different small airlines that chartered planes out into Alaska, taking fisherman and tourists and anyone else with the money away from the troubles of Juneau and back into the outback, back into the country, back into what was called the "real Alaska" by all those crazy promotional ads on the video.

Jaegar sat down to drink his coffee on one of the benches beside the sliding doors that lead to the rental car parking lot and waited. Juneau airport still only had one gate and one baggage claim area, and they were close enough together he could watch them both at the same time. He was, however, unfamiliar with all the entrances and exits to the airport, so he was startled when Bishop Brewan walked up behind him and clapped him on the shoulder and said, "Welcome to the Southeast, brother.

"Oh," he jumped up, almost spilling his coffee. "It's, it's good to see you, Bish." He set his coffee cup down on the bench and gave Rev. Brewan a hug, something that startled Bish. Jaegar had never been a hugger. Was Alaska working its magic already? He smiled. Time would tell.

A century earlier a trip to Juneau would have included a visit to the Mendenhall Glacier. It would have meant visiting Chapel by the Lake in Auke Bay. It would have meant walking along the Bay in Juneau, visiting all the shops. Riding the tram up Mt. Roberts. But anymore those things were only memories in the minds of the oldest Alaskans in the area.

There was no Mendenhall Glacier, not anymore. Chapel by the Lake Church was now Chapel by the Lake Foundation, the largest Christian service nonprofit organization in the state. Commerce in Juneau was more and more every year surpassed by Anchorage, so much that everyone assumed Juneau would soon stop being the state capitol.

Tomorrow Jaegar and Brewan would take the *Taku II* to Kake. Jaegar was going to be in the Southeast for two and a half weeks and planned to accompany Brewan on visits to all the churches in the area, all the EPIC churches at least. It really was going to be, he felt it in his heart, the trip of a lifetime.

Chapter 41

Someone once told Bish that hindsight is always 20-20. He wasn't sure who said it. More and more as the years passed he realized that many of the things he attributed to Grandma Kaye and Aunt Posie had probably not originated with them, or had been mistakenly credited to them because he could not remember where he had really heard them. He hoped that when he got to Heaven the two ladies would not be waiting there with a long list of complaints, telling him they had really never said those things at all.

Still, later when he would look back at Jacob Jaegar's visit to the Southeast, he would wish in hindsight that they had been less busy. It would've been good to spend more time talking and drinking blucaf and less time scurrying from village to village, trying to see everyone and everything. In the clarity of hindsight, Bishop would wonder if Jaegar had somehow known he would not be making this trip again.

Sometimes people do seem to know things that they could not possibly know. Bish was never exactly sure how that happened. Maybe it was insight, or intuition. He did not really believe in clairvoyance or a sixth sense in the way that some people believed in ESP. At best that was nonsense. At worst it was dealing with powers that had best be left alone, most of the time.

Diane was still working her way through Aunt Posie's journals, fascinated simultaneously by the woman's nebbiness and her insights into the community. Aunt Posie was a wise woman, Diane realized, and spending more time with her in Arizona had been a blessing. Because she had known Hoppy since he was a little boy, Posie had been able to help Diane better understand the adult Bishop Bishop. Childhood is a terrible wonderful dangerous thing. It can mold us, Diane understood, or it can meld us. Either way, so many spend the rest of their lives trying to compensate for the first twenty.

Communities also may spend years trying to make up for inadequacies from their early days, or even their early centuries, that often would be best left unattended. No individual or group can change the past. The future is too far away and too vague. Concentrating on the present is always the best. Telling someone, "The past is past," or saying "It's over, get over it" seldom worked, but the sentiments were valid. People did not need to be mired down by things they could not change. Hadn't someone famous called history muck or bunk or something like that?

Diane had lived with a theologian long enough to know that Hoppy would have called this *sanctification*, the lifelong process of getting better and better every day, and becoming more saint like. "We are justified by Christ," she had heard him talking with Jacob Jaegar, and "we are glorified in death, but this sanctification process, this lifelong journey, is the one that occupies us now."

In the days ahead she too would wonder if Hoppy and Jacob had somehow sensed this was Jacob's last trip, that he was soon to be called to a new journey. Diane had never been a maudlin person but she was affected, like her husband, by the extreme light and dark contrasts of the Alaska seasons. She was no stranger to depression.

Before she had moved to Southeast Alaska she thought she understood what SAD was about, but she really had heard very little about Reverse SAD. In Aunt Posie's journals she had discovered accounts of people who seemed especially manic during the long light summer months. Often these were the same people who had been very depressed during the wintertime. Aunt Posie had never used the terms SAD or Reverse Seasonal Affective Disorder, but the symptoms she described in many of her family and friends matched the anecdotal accounts that Diane found online. And it helped her better understand her Bishop.

Hoppy had been a little boy subject to what his Aunt Posie called "mood swings." She had attributed his sometimes sullenness and his temper tantrums and his weeping to his being a "sensitive child." Diane suspected that it was more than that. She was glad he had spent a lot of time away from the Southeast, on Grandma Kaye's farm in Pennsylvania. If that had not been the case, she wondered, would Hoppy even be alive today?

The suicide rate in Alaska, like the suicide rate in the rest of the world had increased steadily as the effects of The Melt intensified, but twenty years ago, actually even 100 years ago, had been over seven times that of the Lower 48. It was not a safe place for children to grow up. Grizzly bears, fishing accidents, the inaccessibility of healthcare, and the strange shifts of season wreaked havoc on young psyches and developing brains. Diane was glad that she and Hoppy had raised their children in slightly more stable places.

Thinking about Jacob who had no family could cheer her and depress her alternately. She was forced to confront again the question that many of the Christian faith had asked for centuries. Was it really that essential for the formation of eternal souls that God allow people such freedoms that they are able to treat each other so badly? Did being made in the image of God have to include the possibility of totally rejecting the love and laws of the God who made us?

Hoppy would say that it did, she thought. He would insist that humans had to have the ability to be very bad if they were to have the ability to be very good. The Rev. Dr. Bishop Bishop Brewan was not a Calvinist in that twisted misunderstood way of so many of those of his grandfather's era. He believed God was in control, ultimately, but he did not believe that the choices were all God's. God offers us salvation, Diane knew her husband would say, but we do not have to accept it. It is never forced upon people. God does not wish for anyone to be evil, but God does not eliminate evil either, because then the creatures He creates in His own image would have their nature diminished. Choice is essential.

Even, Diane sighed, if that choice meant that part of one's life journey is dedicated to trying to ruin the life journeys of others. She knew it was true, but she hated that truth. But all these things, all these thoughts, would be dealt with later.

Later, she would try to gather together tragedy and theology, light and dark, love and hate, and pain and sorrow. Now she sat on the deck of Posie's Perch, sipping her tea, listening to the man she loved and had married converse with his boss, the man who now was probably the closest he had to being a best friend.

She and Hoppy had wondered over the years what their life would be like if he had Jacob Jaegar's job. Would he be more settled? Would life seem more sensible and calmer? Or would it be too complacent?

She really believed that she could live without the intensity and uncertainty that Hoppy seem to thrive on. She could live with a regular schedule, a normal life, but she was not sure that he ever could. Her husband was certainly as intelligent as his boss, and he had the necessary credentials, but, she shook her head sadly to herself, he probably never would have the diplomatic skills that Jaegar's job demanded.

Sitting there listening to Jacob and Bish, she was amazed how optimistic Jaegar was about everything. The older pastors in the Southeast were "seasoned and wonderful," and the new pastors were "living and learning and improving." She knew that Jaegar was practicing the words, the phrases, that he would use when he made his report to the Elder Council, and she understood that he needed to encourage them, to motivate them to continue EPIC's work here in the Southeast, but she knew also that he made the place seem a much rosier picture than it ever could really be. He painted with bright sunlight and left the dark and stark behind.

Later too, in that 20-20 Hindsight Way, she would think about Jaegar leaving the dark and stark behind, and it would make her cry. She wouldn't be sure that the tears were sad tears or happy tears, but they would be real tears, tears of real love for a man who was a real friend to her and to her husband.

Chapter 42

The rain had let up, at least a little, and Muck was very bored sitting in his room behind the kitchen. Nada Dogg had been fussing for the last half hour, whining and scratching at the bottom of the door. Muck sighed and then stood up. It would be easier to take the stupid wolf for a walk then to listen to him any longer. He put the leash on Nada, not because he thought he could actually control the wolf but because it was the law. Unleashed animals were not allowed in Sitka.

Muck was very tired so his brain was sort of on autopilot. He had planned on just going for a short walk around the block with this crazy canine roommate of his, but his legs ignored his brain, and soon he found himself standing outside Teacher's building, waiting and watching and looking at his watch to make certain he was on schedule.

The Teacher came out right on time and headed in the direction that Muck knew he would. Why was he still doing this? He knew what the wolf wanted. That had become intensively more and more obvious every day for the last two weeks. The wolf wanted the Teacher dead. Muck could understand. He had felt that way for quite a while himself. Now, though, he wasn't sure if he wanted to kill the teacher or the wolf more. Was it possible, he asked himself sometimes when he was sure the wolf wasn't listening, was it possible to figure out a way to get rid of both of these nemeses of his life?

James Aaron had never been a young man who liked being alone, but now, hounded by this stupid non-hound, forced to follow physically The Teacher he no longer followed spiritually, being alone sounded better than just okay.

He kept his hood up, not so much to keep the remaining rain off his head, but to help protect him if The Teacher did turn around and see him. Occasionally he wondered why this had not happened already. It must really be a demonstration of how much his former master lived in his own little world. He did not even notice the things going on around him. Somehow that made him just a little bit sad. Maybe it reminded him of his former self?

So on they went, turn after turn, street after street, just like every other night. Muck sighed some more. Was this like what hell was? Doing the same thing over and over for eternity? Making no progress but making instead ruts on the road where his feet trod the same places again and again? It felt a little like hell right now.

Nada Dogg was pulling harder than usual on the leash and it made Muck growl at him, "Nada Dogg, stop it." The wolf just growled back and smiled a little and that sent a slight shiver up Muck's spine. Who really had whom on the leash tonight?

Dishwashing was not the greatest job in the world but it did give Muck a lot of time to think. Mainly these days he thought that he needed a new job that wasn't dishwashing. If he was going to change his life, and he had recently come to the conclusion that he would really rather lose his life then live it year after year like this, if he was going to change his life, he needed more money. And that meant he needed a better job. It might be nice to have an honest job, a job that paid him well for working well. But was there really such a thing? He had heard that there was but he was not sure he'd ever seen any hard evidence to support that dream.

It looked like Teacher was going to follow his normal route now down toward the hatchery. Happy happy joy joy. Muck would get to go home with the stink of fish in his nose again. He pulled back too hard on the leash and Nada Dogg gave him an angry look. Yes, he was going to have to get rid of that dangerous creature before it got rid of him.

The thought of getting rid of a body inevitably took his mind back to that day he had first realized how sick The Teacher had become. Twice before he had helped Teacher bundle the bodies of dead girls into the back of that old pickup, but never before had he seen what happened to the bodies when they were taken back out. He shuddered now, wishing the memories would not return, but they did.

How many birds had there been? As they came pouring down from the sky it seemed at first as if they were thousands, but really there might have only been hundreds or dozens, yet the noise they had made, the screeching and calling and cawing, the hideous almost human but yet inhuman laughter had assaulted his ears so that he covered them and wanted to turn his back and cover his eyes too, but he could not. They had torn at the poor girl's flesh viciously, ripping first off all the soft parts of her body, her eyes and nose and ears and lips and then working their way down her torso. Her fingers and toes were cracked and ripped and carried away. In a few moments only a bloody pile of bones lay glistening in the rain and the boy in his blue bandana knelt, heaving out his guts and his heart.

And Teacher had laughed the entire time, a deep dark chuckling that seemed to come up from his bowels and break forth from his nose and mouth and ears all at once, a laughter that spoke of hate and harm, of a malicious mind destroyed by ambition and arrogance and a total lack of humanity. Muck was not as stupid as everyone thought he was, and he had read about sociopaths and psychopaths, and for a while he had wondered if teacher was one or both of those things. Later, when he woke up at nights, remembering the birds, he was certain Teacher was much worse, some thing, someone, much much worse.

Nada Dogg growled again and Muck gritted his teeth. He had had just about enough of this. He could not take much more.

Chapter 43

Ran the Man sat sipping blucaf at the front corner window of Café Ole across the street from the Sitka Volunteer Fire Department. The stupid kid and his wolf had passed the window three times already. It was time for Ran to move. He signaled the waitress for his check.

"Is there anything else?" She was a cute young thing, and he thought he heard a lot in that question.

"Not today." He smiled.

"Okay, then. Maybe next time?" He was not imagining it.

"I am sure. See you soon, sweetie."

So, he still had it. But did it still have him? Some days he was not so sure. Since he had arrived in Sitka he had stayed away from all of that. His greed in the Lower 48 had shocked even himself a bit. His appetite had been so out of control, at least so out of his control, that it frightened him a little bit. Ran had never been good at cutting back on things. He had tried to reduce his smoking six times before he finally gave up and just quit. It'd been the same with drinking. He discovered he could drink only two ways, excessively or not at all. He was not an alcoholic like his pathetic little cousin. But he was a mean drunk. He had decided, therefore, not to drink at all.

Berth Day Kake

After returning to the Southeast he had thought that might be the best way with the girls too. Maybe no more girls at all would be better, would be the best even. He could not drink without drinking excessively. He could not smoke without smoking too much. Maybe he could not love without hurting either.

But that did not matter now. What mattered now was completing this ambush. Now it was time to get rid of that stupid stupid kid and his stupid stupid Wolf. He paid his check and walked back out into the rain. It was going to be a long evening.

Ran walked downhill from the cafe, down toward the water, following the path James Aaron knew he always took. The boy and his wolf followed.

Ran laughed softly to himself. Why did he call him the boy and his wolf? Didn't auras around them both suggest it was more like the wolves and their boy? There was more than one something inside the lad, maybe even a legion of them. He guessed it did not matter. Soon he would be rid of them both, either way.

At the end of the block he turned left walking down toward the Marine Highway Ferry terminal built on the grounds of what had been Sheldon Jackson University before the Edgecomb Disaster, back when this water had rested several blocks further down, blocks that The Melt and the volcano had teamed up to obliterate. He stopped at the visitors' center next to the ferry terminal and took out his binoculars as he did every time. He wondered if the boy, or the wolf, conjectured about what he looked for. It was just an excuse to make sure they kept up. They were what he was looking for.

In the first couple of weeks that they had followed him, Ran had considered simply confronting them and telling them to knock it off. That's what one reasonable man would've done when followed by another. Ran knew that. But he knew too that they were not reasonable men. They were not ordinary men. And they were not entirely their own agents, were they?

Now, this was better. Better to eliminate the threat now. Better to have it over with.

Someone, certainly a tourist from his umbrella, because nobody in Sitka carried umbrellas, was pulling brochures from the Plexiglas protected information stand outside the ferry terminal. Keeping the binoculars up to his eyes, Ran pretended to watch the horizon until the man moved on, down the boardwalk toward the punk and his puppy.

Ran was not sure how fast the wolf could move. Would he be as speedy as the real wolf, a *normal* wolf he corrected himself, or would he be slower, or would he be faster? He had decided it was safer to assume the wolf was incredibly fast. That was why he carried now both the gun and the knife.

He would kill the wolf first and then the boy and then he would cut himself so he looked like their victim instead of the other way around if police responded too quickly for him to flee. He would only get two shots so they both would have to count, but that did not worry him. In the woods growing up hunting and trapping and tracking, he had learned that it was always the first shot that was most important. If the first shot did not count, you might not get a second. Bears and wolves and things that go bump in the night did not promise you second chances.

He moved on now, passing the terminal, closed because no ferries were due in until early morning, and walked toward the fish hatchery, another newer building replacing the old one the volcano had destroyed. Since the street curved here, he could look across and be certain the dorky duo was following him. They were.

Past the main building of the hatchery, he always turned left and crossed the street heading toward the former site of the historic totem park, a historic site obliterated by the disaster but being restored slowly now as funds became available. Clearly, it was not a priority, he shook his head in disgust, just as the ways and things of his people were never a priority to the invaders.

He always turned left, but not tonight. Instead he ducked behind the large emergency generator between the hatchery and its parking lot and he waited. As he predicted, as he had counted on, dummy and wolfie crossed the road as they always did. Now he was behind them. The hunters had become the hunted.

How many times had he practiced it in his head? How many times had he visualized each movement carefully, controlling his breathing, holding his arms steady, squeezing the trigger, bracing himself against the recoil? He sort of wished now that he had counted. It was not important but it might be interesting.

Enough of that. As the hunters become the hunted reached the other side of the street, Ran the Man stepped out, the large handgun held firmly in front of him at chest height.

"Hey, assholes." He hissed at them and they turned just as he knew they would.

"Say bye-bye."

The wolf was incredibly fast, but the color changes in his aura gave him away. There was a slight hesitation, a momentary confusion and color fluctuation in his glow before he leapt, and the bullet from the gun slammed into his chest before his back feet left the ground. He was dead before the boy's scream escaped his own chest.

Ran smiled now. "Night night, numbnuts." He squeezed the trigger again, savoring the moment a moment too long, seeing the movement in his peripheral vision almost too late.

Later, after the running and the crying and more running, Muck would replay it over and over in his head. Why had that tourist turned around and followed him? What were the pamphlets in his hand? Why had he attacked The Teacher instead of ducking for cover? How had the second bullet missed him when the first had so clearly hit to exactly where the Teacher intended? And why had The Teacher slammed a knife into the tourist's heart over and over again instead of shooting him? And why had the tourist died smiling?

So much of it did not make sense. What had happened to Nada Dogg's body? Why hadn't Teacher followed him and finished him off?

Then, however, there were more immediate concerns. He resisted the impulse to race back to his room and grab his gear. Was he safe now from that maniac? Did he know where he lived? How fast could he get out of town? And how could he be certain he was not being followed? The only thing he could count on was running faster than the old man. So he ran.

Ran the Man did not run. He moved quickly but calmly, dragging the stupid stupid tourist's body behind the generator where he had so recently hidden himself. He left his knife in the body, knowing his gloves had protected him from any possibility of tracing fingerprints. But he kept the gun. He would need it when he caught up with stupid stupid boy.

The shots had been heard, of course. Fifteen minutes later the police found Jacob Jaegar's body behind the generator, but by then the Teacher was back in his room watching television.

Chapter 44

"All of you who sit here today knew Jacob Jaegar. Some of you well, some of you only slightly, but in one way or another Jacob Jaegar affected all of our lives. Most of you knew Jacob as a very calm man, a strong man with firm convictions but a quiet voice and a counseling mind and a loving heart. We will all miss him.

"I first met Jacob when we were both very young and at the seminary here in Pittsburgh. There is an old saying, "Opposites attract," and another old saying, "Birds of a feather flock together," and I believe they are both true, and they both explain why Jacob and I worked so well together for so many years in the fields of the Lord. We were very different and we were very much alike. I only wish I were half as good a man as Jacob Jaegar was, and is, and will always be.

"I don't know how many of you knew that Jacob was a rower. In college and then in seminary too he raced shells along the Allegheny, zipping along the top of the water working those crazy long oars with a frantic speed that made him look like a water bug zooming across the top of a pond. When Jacob was on the water he seemed to be his happiest.

"Jesus told his first followers that there were places for all of them, that he was going to prepare a place for them. I always thought this meant that the Lord loved us enough that he was going to individualize our eternal homes to match our personalities. God's loving Son by and in whom all things were created, according to the gospel of John, knows and understands each of us better than we know and understand each other, and even better than we know and understand ourselves. Therefore, the places he prepares for us must be better than any home we ever had and better than any home we could ever imagine. I am certain that Jacob Jaegar has a place on the water now, a river or a pond, some place where he can zip along rowing as much as he likes, and I'm sure as he does so there is a big smile on his face.

"There is an interesting word used among people who live or work around the water. And that word is *berth*. B-e-r-t-h. The word berth has two meanings. First, it means the place along the dock or wharf assigned to a particular boat. It's the place that the boat is moored on a regular basis, the place that the boat rests when it is not sailing out and about. The second meaning of the word *berth* refers to a bed for a bunk on a boat where sailors can sleep when they are not working, when they finally get a chance to rest. Jacob Jaegar has found his berth now in Heaven. He is resting on the water, taking the Sabbath from his busy time here on earth, resting up, getting ready to do whatever it is God calls him to do next. Today is Jacob Jaegar's *berth* day.

"Today, Jacob Jaegar is in his berth and today's the day that may last for twenty-four hours or twenty-four years or twenty-four centuries. None of us knows. When Jesus was asked when the world would end, he replied that only the father knew. So it would be presumptuous of us to pretend that we know.

"What we do know, however, is that someday Jesus will be back. He made us that promise. Scripture teaches us that all the Saints will also be back. Someday, Resurrection Day, Jacob Jaegar will walk this earth again and sail on the rivers and ponds in a resurrected body, sailing faster than ever before. He will have and we will have a rebirth day. Praise the Lord for that."

The Rev. Dr. Bishop Bishop Brewan sat down beside his wife Diane. She reached over and held his hand. Jacob had been her friend too, but he was in Heaven now and he was fine. She hoped that Hoppy, her husband Bish, would be fine too.

Bish had never had a brother. When he was a boy, his cousin Ran had been the closest thing to a brother he knew. Later, it had been Jacob Jaegar. Now, in many ways he would feel like an orphan. It would be up to her and the girls, up to Ronni and Van, and up to the ElderCouncil to try to fill that gap labeled "brother" in Bish's heart. She hoped they all were up to it.

She would try to convince Bish that it was time now for him to slow down, but she knew this would be a waste of time. Because of what had happened to Jacob, Bish was going to be more determined than ever to fight for the souls of all those folks he had been charged to teach and serve. He would probably die doing it, sooner or later. The best she could do now was try to make it later. The best she could do now was live and love and serve with him.

Bishop saw the tears in her eyes and thought they were for Jaegar not for him, she realized. That was the way it should be. The program said five other friends and colleagues were scheduled to speak at this funeral. Afterwards there would be a lunch at the chapel. This would be an arduous day that they would all get through it because they had each other and because they all knew that it was what Jacob Jaegar would have expected of them.

Wasn't that how it was supposed to work? "What a Friend We Have in Jesus" was one of the songs listed in the program. What a friend they had all had in Jacob Jaegar also. Diane remembered that Jesus had once told his disciples they were not his servants but instead his friends when they followed his commands. That was what they all would do now until they met Jesus and Jacob again. They would follow the Lord and they would be friends, whatever that meant, whatever that took, wherever that led.

ABOUT THE AUTHOR

When Harv Boal first visited Southeast Alaska twenty-five years ago, he instantly fell in love with its people, its geography, and its history. A retired teacher and pastor, Harv tells stories about an Alaska in an alternate reality and timeline where people ignore the past and in doing so imperil the future. Between visits to Alaska and Mexico, Harv resides in rural Pennsylvania with his wife Lynn.

Cochranton Area Public Library

WITHDRAWN

Made in the USA
Charleston, SC
25 August 2015